Divided Loyalties

Lara MacGregor

A Wings ePress, Inc
Historical Romance Novel

Wings ePress, Inc.

Edited by: Jeanne Smith
Copy Edited by: Joan C. Powell
Executive Editor: Jeanne Smith
Cover Artist: Trisha FitzGerald-Jung

All rights reserved

Names, characters and incidents depicted in this book are products of the author's imagination or are used fictitiously. Any resemblance to actual events, locales, organizations, or persons, living or dead, is entirely coincidental and beyond the intent of the author or the publisher.

No part of this book may be reproduced or transmitted in any form or by any means, electronic or mechanical, including photocopying, recording, or by any information storage and retrieval system, without permission in writing from the publisher.

Wings ePress Books
www.wingsepress.com

Published In the United States Of America

Wings ePress Inc.
3000 N. Rock Road
Newton, KS 67114

What They Are Saying About Divided Layalties

Duncan Amberly certainly is attractive and, what is more, manages to say the right things. He likes educated women (good heavens!), he speaks of music…and we wonder if Clarissa's heart will betray her. At the start, it is easy to believe her love will cause her descent into darkness…that this is all a carefully woven romance, but it is more. There is more waiting for young Clarissa; from a dangerous journey to a kidnapping, and before her is a darkness we could not have predicted. What seems a subtle romance actually involves a tangled tale of mystery and intrigues around the war. Shared sorrows unite some, but loyalties and family have a huge role to play here. The unpredictable nature of this story combines with the well-maintained tone and believable characters to keep the interest building throughout. Specifics of the war are perhaps a tad complex, but one need not know the details of the conflict to understand the challenges to various people's loyalties, or how differing loyalties could tear a family apart.

The pace and setting of this historical romance seem perfect. The dialogue is different enough to hint at the year, without being extreme enough to distract. The courtesies of the day are carefully observed (or acknowledged at least, for we must admit that Clarissa is not of the upper classes).

The shop, their 'regulars' and even their goods are all wonderfully appropriate and become a remarkably visible backdrop for much of the tale. The family members—even the remembered sorrows, give wonderful depth to even lesser characters.

Any fan of the historic romance will enjoy *Divided Loyalties.*

—Snapdragon
Long and Short Reviews

Set during the Georgian period while Bonaparte rampages through Europe, this novel shows that MacGregor knows the era, and shares its detail without hampering the storyline. She delivers quite the story of a woman's strength and a man's determination as they search for answers to abduction and espionage. Quite the page turner.

It reads almost like a script as the dialogue takes the reader onto the stage boards and into one's imagination, a new concept of writing that is worth exploring. You'd think it would sink into 'telling,' but it does not, and it takes a talented author to pull it off.

For a good read, this one is worth your while.

—Katherine Pym,
Author of Historical Fiction

Dedication

To my friend Diana, a wonderful historical writer, and my three best historian friends, Marie, Erica, and Stevi. I have learned a lot about history, writing, and friendship from you. Also, this is to my friends in the HisFic critique group, those who helped me with the original version of this book.

* * *

Acknowledgment

For information about Russia during 1812, I mainly used the book *1812: Napoleon's Invasion of Russia* by Paul Britten Austin.

One

North of London 1811

Please, let there be help up ahead.

Clarissa fingered the torn sleeve of the blue-green pelisse draped over the shoulders of her traveling gown. She had trimmed the garment herself more than once in an attempt to make it more fashionable. Beads of red glistened between the ragged edges of the rip. She stared as if at a line of rubies surrounded by turquoise stone, then lowered her arm. Focusing on the blood, though an inconsequential amount, would only worry her brother Gilbert.

With a glance over her shoulder at the unwieldy, old-fashioned coach lurching at an odd angle next to its damaged wheel, she sighed, regretful. At least she and her brother had a nice visit with old friends in Hampstead, friends who had brought them to their home for a luncheon.

Their friends' adolescent son had taken their only vehicle out without notifying his parents, leaving Clarissa and Gilbert without transport home.

The farmer next door from whom they hired the coach gave every proof of his displeasure when Clarissa and Gilbert had returned the horses, sans vehicle.

Vexed with worry, Clarissa gripped her reticule. Questions raced across her mind as she and Gilbert continued up the hill. What if the elements overcame them? What if they ran into unsavory characters?

She shuddered as a groan fell from her lips.

Gilbert laid a kindly hand on her arm. "Do not worry. We'll find help somewhere along this road, and thankfully we'll have no snow in this fog."

She peered through the mist-shrouded way, drawing a breath of moist air. Gilbert's walking stick thudded on the hard ground as they strolled. He kept up with her, despite his lame leg. A thin wool coat stained with mud covered his shoulders. Getting out of the tilted carriage had put him at a disadvantage, and he'd tumbled.

Clarissa's mind continued its anxious questioning. Home, the family business, and their future. What did it all hold?

"Can it concern you if our shop will not continue to prosper? Papa would hate that," she said to cut through the eerie desolation of the quiet road.

"No. Have faith. Our day will arrive. After that, we'll have enough saved so we can move from our rooms above the shop into a fine home with a bit of land. And," he said, "cease living as frugally as we do."

"We shall convince your dear Harriet to venture out with us."

"I should rather suppose coaxing will do much towards it, but we must not forget her nerves. Never stop trying though."

"No. Perhaps I will meet *my* true love, an ambitious clerk or a shopkeeper or someone of that ilk." She shivered, the frigid air seeping into her bones.

"I am perfectly convinced of it," Gilbert said. "A gentleman? I wish you would use a part of our savings for a *modest* dowry and not that pittance."

"And delay the purchase of a pleasant home? I do not care to do that to you and Harriet. Or Mother." *We'd have to give up the majority of the savings we've collected over the years to provide a dowry respectable enough to attract the attention of a fine gentleman.*

"We don't mind."

"We've waited so long, Gilbert. I would not extend the time. I would have your children growing up better than we did."

"I have no children yet. There's time."

"I imagine it will be within a couple of years."

"Clarissa, you are selfless. But—"

"Words of Everett, Mr. *Norwood,* come to mind." She paused before a tree, remembering an attractive young army soldier.

He was twenty, she eighteen at the time of their engagement. He approached her that terrible day, across the counter of her shop, tossing a glance around first. Two customers leafed through books on the far end of the establishment—out of earshot. Mr. Norwood had broken his and Clarissa's engagement and cruelly told her not to pursue action or risk humiliation.

Gilbert's words cut through the memory. "What did Mr. Norwood say to you?"

Hot embarrassment took over. "That no *gentleman* would have me. My origins and my appearance would hinder my prospects." Her arm ceased stinging, and she said a silent thank you. "I wouldn't wish the mortification. I couldn't take another defeat."

"Clarissa—" Gilbert slipped into his old East End accent, making her aware of his concern.

"No," she said tersely. "I would suspect a *gentleman's* motives, should his eye fall upon me."

Aim low, Clarissa, Mr. Norwood had advised, making implications of her humble status and of what she might expect.

Gilbert tapped her arm. "Poor dear. You, like me, may come from low origins, but you're a gem."

Her brother often fed her need to be complimented. Ahead at the junction of two streets rested a Queen Anne mansion, and laughter floated toward them. Clarissa turned to Gilbert.

"Come." He strode faster, bearing down on his cane with each shuffling step.

Spots of brightness appeared further down the lane, interspersed in the dying light of dusk. A line of colorful lanterns cast romantic circles of light onto shadowed areas below. Clarissa gasped at the beauty of it. People in elegant capes and dark great coats skated on a frozen pond.

Gilbert watched the scene wistfully and tossed a glance at his leg. "I wonder what it would be like, had I not been born with this."

"You're strong and could forever keep up with me," Clarissa assured him.

"I suppose you're right."

She turned to observe the skaters. "I don't expect they would help poor folks like us?"

"There's one way to find out." He offered his arm, and she laced hers around it. "You must discover everything, sister!"

They traversed beneath overhanging oak branches and across a crunchy gravel approach. Before the skating pond, she saw *him*: A tall, dark gentleman, wearing the blue and white uniform of a naval officer. His image seized her heart. Her lips parted.

Gilbert touched her arm. "Clarissa, what is it?"

She quivered.

"Are you chilled?"

She turned to face him. "Yes, but it's not that."

"Then what?"

My life has just changed.

She put gloved hands to her nervous stomach in an effort to settle the flips it made.

"Please, Clarissa."

She watched the stranger.

Gilbert followed the direction of her scrutiny. "He has a serious air about him."

"Y...yes." She glanced at her brother before turning back to *him*.

Out of the corner of her eye, she perceived the smart grin on Gilbert's lips. The object of her admiration was deep in conversation with another gentleman, who resembled him with his dark hair and general build, but he did not wear a uniform; instead he was dressed in a frock coat and breeches. He appeared refined, cultivated, and perhaps closely related to the officer, but his features were softer than the officer's, for he lacked the scar on his chin the other had, and he had the general look of a man unused to work. Clarissa thought they must have led distinctive lives, had dissimilar experiences for it to be so.

"Let's ask the naval captain." Gilbert strode forward, and Clarissa fell into step beside him.

Several of the skaters stopped moving on the ice and threw them cold stares as they passed. Clarissa's cheeks heated from unease, the merchant among this glittering company. A few paces in front of their target, they stopped. Clarissa's eyelashes fluttered down. She studied her booted feet.

"Pardon me, gentlemen," Gilbert said. "I'm truly regretful to interrupt your gathering."

"How can I help you?" The deep but sympathetic voice came from the naval captain.

She tipped her head up slightly but didn't meet his eyes.

"Duncan, really, have them escorted away," the man next to him said.

"Wouldn't it be the charitable thing to discover what they want?"

"Thank you, Captain." Gilbert offered a small bow.

"Captain Amberley. At your service."

"Delighted to make your acquaintance. I am Mr. Hale, and may I present my sister, Miss Hale?"

"Delighted," the captain said.

Clarissa curtsied; her heart pounded harder than even when she had walked up that hill. She couldn't believe her reaction to this man, and panic crept into her gut. She had to rein this in fast, for he was a gentleman.

Gilbert whispered, "Clarissa!" not unkindly, but with a tinge of laughter in his voice.

Her chin shot up at her brother's command, and her gaze aligned with the captain's. She quivered with trepidation. Too many people threw curious glances her way, and she resented their rudeness.

Captain Amberley stepped back. "My God." He shook his head. "I beg your pardon."

Her lip trembled. She cared what he thought and the impression she would leave behind. If only a compliment had fallen from his lips.

"It was not my intention to offend you, Miss. It is only that I have never seen eyes of such an extraordinary shade. Forgive me."

Persuaded of his sincerity, Clarissa clasped her lips shut, but his response had troubled her. Did he think her peculiar? As a child, other children had teased her and run from her because of the unusual color of her eyes. Gilbert had once compared them to a turquoise stone.

Captain Amberley glanced down. "I'm sorry. I'm a fool."

"Not at all," she uttered.

The man beside him cleared his throat, and Captain Amberley gestured toward him.

"May I present my brother, Mr. Ewan Amberley, to you?"

"I am pleased to make your acquaintance, sir," Gilbert said, and then to the captain, "Our hired old coach hit a pothole—"

"What?" Mr. Amberley scoffed. "Have we met?"

"I don't believe so. Have you ever been to Hale's Emporium on Oxford Street? I own it."

Mr. Amberley smirked.

He's rude for a gentleman, Clarissa thought.

"Shopkeepers," the rude one muttered mockingly.

"Ewan!" the captain snapped before addressing Gilbert again. "I assume you require assistance?"

Mr. Amberley glared at him and strode away.

"If it would please you to offer it," Gilbert responded.

"Of course." The captain didn't take his eyes off Clarissa.

Mr. Amberley returned with a pretty blonde woman, arguably five years older than Clarissa, and dressed in a fine gown. Captain Amberley inhaled deeply.

A smug smile brightened his brother's face. "May I present Miss Elizabeth Donovan?"

Clarissa noted the woman's excellent dress and coat, her expensive velvet hat, and the glittering diamonds at her ears. The woman lowered long lashes over a suggestive brown-eyed gaze and directed it to the captain. Clarissa wasn't dim-witted. She knew this dazzling woman had to be Captain Amberley's mistress.

"She has recently arrived," Mr. Amberley added, "and wanted to see you, brother."

This struck a chord of sadness in Clarissa, and she swallowed the lump in her throat. The captain had a woman. Clarissa snapped out of it. What was she thinking, allowing herself to be stung with irrational jealousy?

The captain clenched his jaw and bowed curtly. "If you will excuse us. Ewan, see to our guests. You're the host of this gathering, as it stands. Since I've only arrived home moments ago, I shall hardly be missed."

"Duncan—"

"I'll return shortly." He turned to Clarissa and her brother, gesturing. "Follow me, Mr. Hale, Miss Hale." He strode forward angrily.

You cut her, the snub of a lifetime.

Clarissa's mind streamed with possible explanations, trying to make sense of this. *She isn't your mistress?* Despite herself, hope sprang within her heart.

The captain led the way across the lawn, and as Clarissa trailed behind, she glanced over her shoulder at Mr. Amberley whose lip curled with derision. Turning her attention ahead, she smiled.

Woods stretched behind a fetching stone two-story mansion, which emerged from the mist. Relatively new, possibly it had been built late in the last century, and the heathland around it added to its charm. A carriage driveway curved around its front.

What a beautiful home, she thought again.

They made their way up three wide steps, and a footman opened the door.

"Please find Phineas," the captain said to him. "I'm going to accompany Mr. and Miss Hale."

The footman bowed and strode away to fulfill his task.

"Phineas is my coachman."

"This is your home?" Gilbert asked with awe.

Impressed, Clarissa held onto her brother's arm.

"Yes," the captain answered. His lips curved into a smile.

"Pardon me, Captain, are you titled?" Gilbert asked.

Clarissa bit her lip, embarrassed.

"No."

She gazed down.

"Miss Hale?" Tenderness softened the dashing captain's voice.

A sigh escaped her. The alluring emerald eyes of a romantic sea captain would forever haunt her.

He regarded her. "Would you care for refreshments?"

"No," Gilbert responded. "Thank you."

"And you, Miss Hale?"

"No," she muttered and curtsied.

The footman returned with another man.

"Phineas, my new friends require assistance. We will escort them home."

"Certainly. Right away."

He turned to Gilbert. "Where to?"

"Oxford Street, if you wouldn't mind." He gave further directions.

They followed the captain down the outside steps and along a path. Clarissa hummed, nervous in his presence. Afore long, they and the good captain were riding in his coach led by four excellent chestnut horses. She sat next to Gilbert and opposite Captain Amberley, her attention on her glove's bow.

"Pardon me, but you did not have to accompany us," Gilbert said.

"It's my pleasure to do so. I'm curious."

Oh no. Clarissa's mind spun with the implication in his tone. She'd heard it previously in gentlemen's voices. The captain seemed interested.

This can't be happening. She would not be a *mistress*, for surely that's what he was considering, if she were not mistaken, she in her re-trimmed clothes escorted by a brother in a muddy coat. The familiar sense of humiliation and hurt sneaked inside.

Gilbert reclined against the plush velvet coach seat. "What do you wish to know?"

Clarissa detected suspicion in his voice.

"Tell me about your establishment."

"We sell books, antiquities, and curiosities from across the globe. My sister purchases our stock, items of excellent quality."

She gulped and didn't speak out against her discomfiture, embarrassed by Gilbert's pride in her abilities, and believing her cleverness was not a way to impress the typical gentleman.

Gilbert continued. "We house the oddest things you might encounter and are acquainted with an amateur inventor." He clapped once, proud in a boyish fashion. "If you pay us a visit, we will find something in our shop you cannot live without."

Clarissa froze, anticipating a polite comment that masked a refusal. A half-grin marked the captain's face.

Gilbert added, "The first item will be free of charge, of course, as payment for your kindness."

"That's not necessary, Mr. Hale," their benefactor said, surprising her. "You owe me nothing."

Gilbert smiled.

"But, thank you." Captain Amberley regarded Clarissa. "You may find me frequenting your establishment. I'm fond of reading."

Yes, your voice says so much. You are intrigued with me. Maybe hoping to steal some pleasure? She glanced out the window.

They passed a watering hole for exerting horses traveling the hill. Everett Norwood's image came prominently to her mind. When he had broken the news that he'd changed his mind and no longer wished to be tied to her, something inside of her changed. Her shoulders stooped as she remembered.

You are too beautiful to take as a wife, to trust with other men. Aim low, Clarissa. For only a clerk could respect you.

Had he spoken those words to hurt her?

But why did you ever propose?

Your beauty blinded me initially. I find I can't live with the anxiety it would bring me. I've been in this shop and have seen an appreciative eye cast upon you from many a man.

She fought the burn of tears, wanting Captain Amberley and wishing she had not met him.

~ * ~

Clarissa took a seat opposite Gilbert in the simple but pretty dining room above their shop and poured tea. Moonlight peeked in through soft yellow curtains. Candles brought a glow to the room. Quaint, but clean and homey, it was their residence *for the present.*

"She's asleep," Gilbert said, referring to his wife.

Droplets of hot tea spilled onto the table. Clarissa set the pot down and dabbed at the spots with a cloth.

"That was the oddest encounter with the good captain, Clarissa. He was staring at you the entire time even while he was conversing with me."

She brought her cup to her lips. "His eyes were like emeralds. His dark-brown hair—"

"Yes." The sarcasm fell from his lips. "What of it? Women."

She didn't respond.

"Ah, I see. You were charmed by him."

"Gilbert."

"Admit it!"

"I will not!"

He tapped his walking stick three times on the wooden floor, his tone playful. "I suppose he's pushing thirty."

"And I'm twenty, old enough for a man of his years."

"Aha, I knew it! You're considering him. You're hoping he has no wife."

"He doesn't."

He tilted his stick against the table and poured milk into his tea. "You are convinced of this? How?"

"I just am."

He took a swallow and replaced the cup in its saucer. "Women's intuition." He winked. "I'm sure he has a dark, mysterious past." His voice became theatrical. "He's probably seen things you have never even read about."

She might have chuckled had she not been mesmerized by the recent memory of the man who had taken her by storm, the man she feared would disturb her dreams and test her resolve.

"What do you mean? Tell me, my brother, you with your wild imagination."

"He has probably found himself in trouble due to his heroism." He grasped his cane.

She glanced at him, and he continued with his story.

"He was spared in battle with the French, so he could return, sweep you off your feet, and make you say, 'Everett who?'"

"Oh, you."

"His brother, you noticed? Captain Amberley did not hide his concern. And that woman he cut." He glanced down. "Well, thank God for that because of the way he regarded you. It was stark interest and yet respectful—"

She cut him off. "I wonder how the captain received that small scar along his jaw." Her voice was reflective as she recalled him.

"Probably in combat, in a romantic battle on a large ship going down in flames, as Boney's men blasted it with cannon. He was probably the only survivor, but not for lack of trying to save his entire crew unaided." He continued with flourishing tones, "Imagine him floating in the middle of the ocean on a piece of driftwood, near death, no sooner than being rescued by the king's men, then given honors for heroism."

She'd play along to forget her distress. "Do you think he used a sword?"

"What?"

"To try to save his entire crew as Boney's men jumped onto his ship?"

He laughed.

"That is sufficient."

"You're in love! Unbelievable. Now I shall tease you mercilessly and have good reason for doing so."

"Stop. I told you what type of man I hope to marry."

He gestured with nonchalance. "Yes, yes."

"Are you really three and twenty?"

"Why?"

"Because you conduct yourself as a child would!"

He shrugged. "You've forever enjoyed the playful nature of our relationship."

"I won't deny I like him, considerably."

"I sense he thought it charming."

"To what do you refer?"

Gilbert pointed to a spot near the outer corner of her right eye. "Your birthmark."

"My tear-shaped freckle."

"Painted silver as it is, it's exquisite."

"I had to do something. It's prettier silver, as if it is a tear, and represents the goings-on of my heart."

"I think it enhances your beauty. It gives you a perpetual charm, as if you were an angel crying for the sad state of humanity."

"You appreciate it, but you're my brother. I suppose the color of my hair is just the thing, too." She twirled a loose stand of light brown hair around her finger.

"As a matter of fact, yes. Stop fretting. You are too afraid of rejection. Too suspect of people's motives. You truly are all I've ever said you are, clever and beautiful."

Melancholy tightened her throat as she thought of Mr. Norwood again. "You are a good, dutiful brother."

He tapped her wrist resting on the table. "You are so vulnerable."

I yearn to be loved. "I want a husband who will appreciate my mind."

He offered unspoken compassion. His look told her he'd be her protector until the end of time.

She twisted a blue-green ribbon from the bonnet resting at her side. "Why did Mr. Norwood *really* leave me, Gilbert? He advanced excuses. Do you suppose he was embarrassed? He says it was my beauty rendering me untrustworthy, but I fear he wasn't enchanted with my inquisitive mind."

"But the captain seemed different."

Clarissa half-wanted Captain Amberley to pursue her. She hoped to accept him with no questions asked concerning his *true* intentions, to assume they were honorable. Quite to her consternation, her other half prayed she'd meet a nice shopkeeper she could be confident appreciated her for her intelligence, a man not resenting being tied to his social inferior, for they'd both be working class.

Gilbert smiled at her as though the summer sun cut through gray clouds. "I mean for you to be happy, and he makes you glow. I see something in you others don't. You are capable of great self-sacrifice and occasionally perform mad and astonishing actions."

"Really now. Don't exaggerate."

"Frankly, I'm worried you'll sabotage your own happiness with an alarming decision you might make, and I'll never allow that to happen."

She considered him, thinking of their beloved father. Gilbert resembled him except for his dark blue eyes. Clarissa had been the offspring to inherit their father's extraordinary bright bluish-green eyes.

Papa, I'll never let you down. Gilbert can't do my job the way I can. I'm the one who finds the uncommon treasures that bring people into the shop. Gilbert's strengths lie elsewhere.

She made up her mind. If the captain came into Hale's Emporium, taking her by surprise and pursuing her, she would surely turn him away, for she wouldn't sacrifice her honor or dreams...honor if he searched for a mistress, and dreams if he aspired to having a wife. She knew a gentleman would never allow her to work.

Two

The next evening, Clarissa moved away from the pile of books she had positioned on the main counter. Gilbert scanned them. A few customers lingered, perusing the varied items for sale on oaken shelves.

The bell at the door tinkled. Clarissa stole a glance, bracing herself. She had been thinking of the captain. Mrs. Lankston, who owned the millinery next door, walked in, and Clarissa sighed from both relief and disappointment.

She was a woman of middling years, and today a violet gown encased the hat merchant's plump figure. She pushed stray locks of curly copper hair under her purple tall bonnet then weaved her fingers around ribbons, buckles, two white feathers, a pink flower, and a bunch of grapes, as if checking to see if all were in their proper position. She adored the flamboyant hats of her own creation. The talented hat maker waved a small book.

"Mr. Hale, Miss Hale, good afternoon." Her voice rang with a singsong quality.

Gilbert passed by Clarissa, grinning. "We are soon to be honored with today's odd lesson," he muttered.

Clarissa faced their interesting neighbor. "Good day, madam."

14

Gilbert proffered a slight bow. "Mrs. Lankston, good day to you. How may I be of service?"

"Hmm." Mrs. Lankston strolled around and dragged her finger over several books. "Amusing myself."

"In that case, madam, do continue. Don't hesitate to call on me if you have any questions."

"Thank you."

"Mrs. Lankston?"

She looked at him inquiringly.

"Usually you have such interesting stories for Clarissa's and my amusement."

"Not today. I brought a gift for your wife."

"Oh?"

Mrs. Lankston gave him the volume, and he took it, scanning its cover.

"It's a volume of original watercolors."

"Thank you." Gilbert opened the book, and Clarissa peered at it briefly.

"It is lovely," Clarissa said. "Thank you on behalf of my sister-in-law."

"My pleasure." She tossed a glance at Gilbert. "Good day to you both."

"Good day." Gilbert bowed again, slightly.

"Good day," Clarissa said.

After their friend and neighbor had left, Clarissa stepped to the curtain that divided the shop from the rear, where the stairs led to their rooms. "I'll peek in on Harriet." She slipped behind the velvet hangings and climbed narrow, creaky stairs. At the top, she knocked on the first door to the right. "It's me."

"Come in."

She entered her brother and sister-in-law's rooms, shutting the door behind her. The blonde ringlets framing Harriet's large blue eyes and alluring face evoked mild envy, for Clarissa disliked her own mousy brown hair. However, Harriet was her closest friend, and she loved her.

"Lemon is a good color for you." Clarissa admired Harriet's dress, protected by an apron.

"Thank you." Harriet's attention remained on the canvas. The paintbrush in her left hand remained suspended as she rested between strokes.

Clarissa was forever amused when she saw this because Harriet used her right hand to do everything else. The brush passed over the paper with grace. Tiny bricks of watercolors rested to her left, the red brick conspicuously absent. Harriet thought red was bad luck. Clarissa walked round and peered over Harriet's shoulder. A picturesque landscape of watery shades came to life under a genius's skillful ministrations.

"It's wonderful!" Clarissa gasped and took a seat next to her.

Harriet offered a weak smile. She returned her attention to her painting, her brush dabbing at a blue brick.

"Tell me what happened to you during the time you were... missing, finally."

The brush froze.

"Harriet, you can trust me. And if you tell me, I'll tell you something."

Harriet lowered the brush. "Why do you pursue this?"

"Because you are precious to me, and I wish to help you, for you to be well again and come shopping with me. We might even venture to the theater."

"Let's discuss happy memories." Sadness underlined Harriet's voice, sending worry through Clarissa. Was she ever going to be herself again?

Clarissa needed tolerance and patience to help Harriet. "Remember the dog that chewed through his rope? We were children walking home..."

"Oh my, Clarissa, how brave Gilbert was!"

Clarissa recalled her brother at that younger age and mimicked his voice, pointing her finger up and over toward the wall, imagining a lofty tree. "Girls, climb that tree!' She used her normal voice to recall the rest of the story. "We raced up an oak like monkeys and were out of harm's way. The mangy creature charged Gilbert, but he stood his ground." She tapped her fingertips together. "Of course, he can't run fast due to his leg. Remember, the dog was upon him?"

"Yes, yes. Gilbert jumped on him to subdue him and scrambled for the rope in the dirt." Harriet smiled. "I recall every detail. He got the rope around the dog's neck, not too tightly, not to hurt him."

Clarissa smiled in return, happy to see a little light appear on Harriet's countenance. "I was full of excitement when we jumped from that tree and ran after him. Then he took the stubborn dog to the owner and pounded on the door, shouting his complaints."

"I fancied your brother for a long time, but it was his courage that impressed me. What of this captain that Gilbert spoke of?"

Those words cut through her like a carriage's wheels through mud.

"What's wrong? Gilbert told me about your encounter, that you were 'indescribably charmed by a handsome naval captain'."

"I..." Clarissa gulped. Miserable, she slouched. "I am unreasonably attracted to him, but..."

"But what?"

"It isn't strictly appearances, well, you see, he looked at me, and I saw something."

"I don't understand."

"The look spoke to me of promise in a way which I've never seen. I care for him, but I'm confused. It doesn't make sense. I've happened upon him only once and *desire* for him to return." She gestured to emphasize her words. "I wish that more than anything, but I wouldn't have him if he showed interest. I only hope to face him with dignity and strength should he keep his word and come to the shop. And yes, I'm sure he won't be coming to search the books. I'm not dimwitted."

"But, Clarissa..."

"He's a gentleman. He might only desire me as a mistress. I will go to my future husband as a maiden, shop clerk that I am." Clarissa realized she should speak of something else. "A gentleman is not likely to wish for a shopkeeper as a wife."

"Indeed not," Harriet said. "Tell me about business."

"Oh, yes. I acquired a suit of armor, circa twelve fifty."

"Really? The cost must have been high," Harriet said.

"Yes, but I have a buyer for it. A collector of medieval pieces. He came to the shop looking. I told him I had connections and might be able to procure his request."

"I'm impressed."

"Thank you. I receive the oddest requests at times and have become expert at acquisitions."

Harriet grinned. "It helps to be acquainted with an amateur inventor."

"Ah, Mr. Wells. Yes, he provides us with interesting oddities for our shop. His strange little inventions sell well. I fancy his teeth cleaner. He made me a custom designed one and promised that if I use it regularly, I shall keep my teeth for decades."

"People travel a distance for the unique things we offer in our little family enterprise," Harriet added.

The door creaked open, and in limped Gilbert, greeting them both. "My dear," he said to Harriet.

She went into his outstretched arms.

"Is that chicken pie I smell?" He sniffed and looked across the room at the stove.

"Your favorite. We'll have soup and cod to go with it, asparagus as well. Then apricot tarts and fruit."

"Mm."

Gilbert took a seat, and Clarissa and Harriet served the food.

During the meal, Clarissa considered the members of her family, so grateful. These two loved her, as she did them. She only regretted the passing of her father. Their mother, who shared Clarissa's rooms with her across the small corridor, was currently visiting friends in the country.

Clarissa observed the low conversation between them and drew within herself.

Clarissa, my love...

Captain Amberley longing to kiss me.

"Clarissa? That was funny, was it not?"

She shifted. "I fear I was not attending."

Gilbert turned to Harriet. "She didn't hear me, and it was funny. Clarissa is intrigued with something rather...interesting."

"Gilbert!" Clarissa laughed but didn't deny it.

"The captain came around moments ago."

Clarissa's breath caught in her throat. "Oh?"

Gilbert's brow crinkled. "I asked him."

Her blood pulsed through her veins with force, and her face flushed. "Wh...what have you asked him?"

"What are his intentions with you?" He pushed his chair back with his feet and spread his legs out in front of him, satisfied.

"And?"

"He told me his intentions were to court you. I told him he needed permission first. He asked to speak to our father. I informed him Father had passed away, and I was your legal guardian, so the good captain asked for *my* permission to court you."

Clarissa bounded to her feet.

He gestured. "Remember what Father spoke of near the end."

She swallowed hard. Her father told his son to not allow any young man who showed interest in Clarissa to court her unless Gilbert first approved of him. He regretted he had told Clarissa, but she was innocent, and he needed his son to protect her and so stated in his will...if she refused, she was not to have anything to do with the shop, which he knew she treasured.

"And...and you told him *no*, did you not?"

He curled his fingers around his walking stick and tapped it on the floor three times as he regularly did when happy. "I told him *yes*. You're captivated with him. I sense how you care for him. Frankly, I'd approve whether he were a farm laborer or a duke. It matters not when you feel so strongly about him, provided he treats you with consideration and respect. I'll have him investigated, but I have a good hunch."

She moved away from the table and paced, biting her lip. "But," she said, "it doesn't make sense. Why me?"

"Clarissa? You're *beautiful*. How often must you hear it?"

She stopped pacing and glanced at Harriet who was smiling. Clarissa glared at Gilbert. "I'm below him." *Tell me why I'm not.*

He scoffed.

"And you don't find it odd a gentleman of his position would want me...as a...as a..." The air around her grew thicker with her disbelief. "Wife?"

"He must have been struck by cupid's dart. Perhaps he's afraid as charming as you are, another man would marry you soon."

"He'd make me resign my work. I can't accept that."

"Gilbert told me how he has affected you. He'll erase what that...man did to you." Harriet's tone failed to disguise her distaste. "Proposing marriage only to break it off was disgraceful."

"Harriet, I doubt it can be love on the captain's part, and that's what I long for."

"It will be, be assured. You are the dearest creature alive."

Gilbert drew her attention back to him. "He's wealthy, he's a gentleman, and I believe he would treat you honorably. Give him a chance. It's what you yearn for. He's not titled so would be allowed to marry you without issue."

"B...but the matter of my dowry."

"Bah! I told him what we could provide, and he responded with due respect he didn't require it."

Harriet's face glowed with delight. "It really may become love."

"He's coming for cards tomorrow evening."

Clarissa gripped her chair.

~ * ~

Rigid in her chair, Clarissa sat next to Harriet, awaiting the two men's arrival. The clock ticked on the mantelpiece, and the loud sound reverberated through the silent room. Gilbert's laughter came from behind the door.

Clarissa watched the entrance as it opened, and the captain entered the room. Cold fear rendered Clarissa unable to move, caught in his stare. He took a few steps and offered his hand. She inched up from her chair.

He bowed. "Miss Hale."

Gilbert stepped forward. "Captain Amberley, my wife, Mrs. Hale."

The captain bowed, and Harriet winced.

"Harriet?" Gilbert asked.

"Pardon me." Harriet offered a clumsy curtsy and turned to Gilbert and muttered. "I...am unwell, Gilbert."

Gilbert took her elbow. "My dear?"

She stumbled, pale, and Gilbert steadied her. Clarissa brought a chair for her, and Harriet sat.

"Shall we postpone the evening?" Gilbert said.

"No, no, do not." Harriet's lips curved into a strained smile.

"All right," Gilbert said.

"Would you like a refreshment?" Clarissa asked. She glanced at a pier table where port wine, sherry, tea, fruit, and cheese rested on a salver.

"Tea, if it's no trouble," Harriet answered.

"And you, Captain, Gilbert?" she asked the men.

"What are you having?" the captain asked.

"Tea for me," Clarissa answered. "I'm going to make it for Mrs. Hale."

"Then that's what I'll have," the captain said.

"And I," Gilbert added, winking at her.

Clarissa opened the mahogany tea caddy and mixed her favorite blend of teas. She poured boiling water into the teapot and allowed it to sit briefly to warm the pot, turning to offer a smile to Harriet. Clarissa glanced at the fine-looking gentleman sitting near Gilbert. Gilbert had situated a flip top card table near him. He chatted with the captain about the latest political happenings. Captain Amberley glanced away from him to Clarissa. Goose bumps of pleasure zipped up her arms. She reached for the water and poured it into a bowl. With care, she put the tea into the warmed pot and poured boiling water over it. While it steeped, she considered the captain.

"Thank you for having me," he said.

"Of course. Which games do you prefer? Loo, Whist?"

"I enjoy various games. Those, Piquet, Vingt-et-un."

"We can play them all!" Gilbert's voice rang with cheer.

The captain chuckled lightly. Clarissa retrieved four teacups and strained out the tea leaves while pouring with a strainer over each.

"Would you like milk or sugar?" she asked the flushed Harriet.

"No."

Clarissa passed her a tea, and Harriet, trembling, took a sip. Clarissa saw pain in her strained features.

"Go rest, Harriet. I insist." She turned to the captain. "You understand?"

"Of course." He glanced at Harriet and offered a slight nod.

Clarissa helped her out of her chair and observed her making her way on shaky legs to the door that led her to a private room. She glanced at her brother and saw the concern there. He seemed to recover his cheer with a forced smile when he noticed Clarissa studying him.

Captain Amberley reached for his cup and took a sip. "Thank you. It's good." He glanced at the table and reached for the book Clarissa had laid there earlier in passing. "*Charlotte. A Tale of Truth*. What's this about?"

"Oh, I like it. It's popular in America," Clarissa answered. "It shows the need for better female education, a guide of what not to do with one's life. I prefer books on the subject of women. And I believe women should be educated."

He raised his brow. "Indeed?"

"Does the idea disturb you?" Gilbert asked.

The captain shifted. "No, it does not. I believe the same."

"Really?" This was an excellent sign.

"Yes, Miss Hale. I'm afraid I may have an odd taste. I appreciate a woman with whom I could hold a conversation. I have traveled extensively, and I value things of exotic origin. It is too common for women to be undereducated or at least feign to be. I find it distasteful."

"You are not repelled by a woman who appreciates she is educated and uses her learning wisely," she said.

"Each time I encounter a woman courageous enough to be proud of her learning, I smile in admiration and encourage her deeper into thoughtful conversation. Women bring an interesting perspective to issues that men don't offer. An intelligent woman is a pleasure to converse with. A woman who makes me think is an even greater pleasure."

Gilbert spoke up. "Our father was of the same opinion, seeing to it my sister's education matched mine in every respect."

"Your father was a discerning man?"

"Yes. His cousin was a man of means and allowed us to be tutored with his own children. He also gave us access to his excellent library. Our father, himself tutored with his cousin, would give us a situation to contemplate and have us converse using the different schools of classical logic. We learned to be persistent in pursuit of understanding. He positioned us against each other. We were both always determined to win. I would not offer her any quarter, or she would cut me to pieces."

Embarrassment flickered through Clarissa, but she was grateful Gilbert had spoken up on her behalf. She could discover if the captain was right for her. Oh, how she went back and forth when it came to him. With luck, Gilbert wouldn't tell him of their truly humble origins, and the small inheritance that enabled their father to elevate them into the merchant class.

The captain seemed to hold her in high regard if his gaze was any indication. Suddenly, modesty overcame her. Sometimes her brother was outrageous, but goodness, she loved him. With a certain look from her, he seemed to take the hint and trailed off.

"What are you schooled in, sir?" she asked.

"The classics, of course. I attended Cambridge and graduated early."

"One of the best universities," Gilbert said.

"In the Royal Navy, I learned seamanship, as you must have supposed. I was only a boy when I stepped onto my first ship, educated already. A number of the crewmembers were resentful of me. I worked particularly hard to prove myself, my worthiness to be a sailor. I had the opportunity to hone my fighting skills early on because I was constantly being pushed around in the beginning."

Images of a valiant fighter flowed through her mind. Conceivably, he fought French officers in close-range combat, a blade sweeping in front of him as he struggled for his life.

"Because you walked on that ship with an education, and you were so young," Gilbert said.

"Exactly. My effort to do exceptionally well, to prove I had the ability to thrive on the sea, earned me promotions. My willingness to jump into battle with concern only for the safety of the crew, earned me the respect of the men. Now I'm retired and running the family estate." He looked at Clarissa. Lowering her eyes, she smiled.

"What else would you recommend from your shop?" he asked. "I fear, or rather, I'm delighted I cannot name everything you have on display on your shelves. Fascinating."

"The inventions of a friend of ours, but you will notice an abundance of old novels. But sir, you are an officer. Perhaps an antique sextant would be to your liking?" she suggested.

"That would do well. Thank you."

"Where have you traveled? America?" she asked.

"No. Possibly, I will travel there in the future. It might be some time though. Trouble is brewing."

"I may visit there as well. I have American publisher friends."

"Why were you in uniform when we first became acquainted with you?" Gilbert chimed in.

"His Royal Highness requested it. He wanted me to brief a few people in politics and asked me to wear my uniform. He thought I would be more authoritative. When destiny first brought you two and me together, I had only just arrived at home to relieve my brother as host."

"You're acquainted with the regent?" Gilbert asked.

"The necessities of war. I did specific work whilst I served, which caught the attention of royalty."

Gilbert raised his brow. "Might you elaborate on those things?"

"Not at this time. Perhaps later." He looked at Clarissa. His lips curved into a lazy smile. "Who are you two?"

"Us?" Surprise tinged Gilbert's tone. "You understand we are the Hales, brother and sister."

"No, that's not what I meant."

"Merchants?"

"I find myself intrigued." His gaze landed on Clarissa again. "There is an unusual quality regarding you both."

She and her brother exchanged astonished looks.

"I will discover your magic yet."

"There's nothing magical concerning us, I assure you," Clarissa stated.

"I'm not so sure. I have a marvelous sense about you. I remember defeating my first French ship as a captain, *et il était merveilleux*. It was wonderful. My instincts tell me much."

"*Je comprends*," Clarissa muttered, having practiced her French with Harriet earlier that day as she often did.

"*J'ai apprendu le français pour servir mieux dans les militaires contre Bonaparte*. I learned French to serve better in the military against Bonaparte."

"Yes," Clarissa responded. "Speaking the language of your enemies would indeed help you to serve better."

"How utterly impressive you speak French," the captain said.

Clarissa frowned. "Why? Because I am a shopkeeper?"

He sat up straighter. "No, not at all! You are actually the only person I am acquainted with outside of the military and some of the nobility that speaks the language."

"The language is musical to me. I first chanced on it when tutored with my brother and cousins, but Gilbert skipped most of the French classes."

"Why did you ask earlier who we are?" Gilbert asked.

"I find myself intrigued. I've never been so thoroughly charmed by a merchant," he said to Clarissa.

"Sir, do not underestimate us or condescend..." Gilbert said.

"You do not understand. I am a merchant myself. I have had the most fulfilling and dazzling friendships with Italian shopkeepers, had my life saved by an English man of commerce turned sailor. I have listened to the most fascinating tales told by African merchants...I was trying to say..."

"I think I understand now. You have encountered people of small business, and we are the most unusual?" Gilbert asked.

"The most charming."

"You are merchant class, like us, but we're at the low end, and you're at the high-end," Gilbert continued.

"I wouldn't say that. Your enterprise appears to be prosperous. It's certainly unique and inviting."

"It's our only shop. How many do you have?"

"We deal with horses, and we have a few of the finest ones."

"Captain," Gilbert used his plainest-speaking voice. "What of you and your *background*?"

Oh my goodness. Clarissa's cheeks heated.

Captain Amberley drummed his fingers on his thigh. "My father made his fortune in trade, up north. He exchanged his factories for land and provided us with the right education to erase our northern accents."

"You're not the younger son?"

"No."

"But you're in the Navy," Gilbert stated. "Or were."

He straightened his posture. "I'm..." He hesitated, and sadness flickered in the form of lowered shoulders. "...now the eldest."

"Captain?" Gilbert asked.

"I lost two brothers, older than me, one in the army, and the eldest...He died of natural causes, a condition he carried since birth. We lost him at the age of thirty."

"I'm sorry," Gilbert said.

Clarissa offered her sympathies.

The captain nodded his thanks. "After my father died, I returned home from the Navy to run the estate. Ewan was doing that, not being the type to join the church as a profession, and I'm afraid he wavers on how to spend his time. Possibly the law..." he drifted off. "Certainly not the clergy, no, not for him." A soft chuckle spilled from his lips. "My father made his fortune and bought this estate when I was a lad, bringing us into the gentry."

"Captain, it is my intention to buy land as well. We invest or save most of our profits in the hope of someday buying a nice home," Gilbert said.

"Tomorrow, I'll come to purchase a selection from your stock. Would you choose them for me, Miss Hale? Perhaps a book from America. I trust your judgment."

"I'd be delighted." She glanced down and saw a yellow ribbon on the floor, Harriet's. Concern came over her. "If you would excuse me, I'm concerned about my sister-in-law."

"Captain, would you mind? I would like to peek in on my wife." Gilbert then glanced at Clarissa. "I'll do it."

"Of course," the captain said.

Gilbert stood and strode across the room, leaving the door to the next open after he entered it.

Clarissa faced the captain. He sat back, relaxed.

"Do you enjoy music, Miss Hale?"

"Oh, immeasurably. Not that I've attended many performances. I have no time, and we are saving our money." She took a sip of her fragrant black tea.

"Have you got a preference?"

"I've never heard his compositions, but what I've read of Beethoven interests me. I should someday hope to actually hear what I've read about!"

"You're enchanting."

Her cheeks heated. "The tale behind his third symphony is interesting."

"How he had originally dedicated it to Boney, being under the impression that the general intended to sustain democratic and republican ideals."

"He was so disappointed later that he violently scratched out the name Bonaparte on his composition." She gestured. "Father knew."

"Pardon?"

"I was thirteen, Gilbert sixteen. Father approached us asking how we supposed Beethoven felt on the subject of old Boney's behavior of late, his imperial ambitions. Father told us he thought Beethoven would un-dedicate his symphony. I agreed with this assessment, but Gilbert didn't. Father had us debate our sides for an hour." Light laughter spilled from her lips.

The captain remained sitting back. "Your laughter resembles music."

Her smiling lips parted.

He watched her with respect. "I would enjoy taking you to performances. Would you like that, Miss Hale?"

"I...yes. Thank you."

"Fill your life with music."

"Captain..."

"Make you smile."

"I...do you laugh often? Because it's something Gilbert and I endeavor to do daily."

"No, as a matter of fact, I do not. My brother says I'm boring and humorless. I foresee that changing."

"Would you have any interesting tales of the sea to share?"

He sat up straighter. "You'll hear them?"

"Yes."

His face lit with a smile. "Ewan rolls his eyes when I tell of an adventure. My mother listens with tolerance. I will have you to supper and tell you my best stories."

"Sounds lovely. What is your mother like? Will she be in attendance?" She sipped her tea.

"Yes. And she's a dear. Scottish. My father first encountered her doing army business in Scotland and fell in love with her. Her father was Laird, and my English father had to prove himself and promise to name a son after him. I was the lucky one to receive the name Duncan. Grandfather liked me best."

"How nice."

"What of your mother, Miss Hale?" He tasted from his tea cup.

"She is visiting friends in the country, but we received a note only yesterday telling us she's been invited to travel. She's a fine woman, a gentle spirit."

"How could she not be, from what I've seen of her children?"

"Thank you."

"May I be bold?"

She shivered. "Yes."

"I have traveled and have been introduced to countless men and women, but never in my journeys have I met the woman who gives my heart pause, until now." He said the last two words in a near whisper.

Gilbert returned and approached Clarissa. "She wants to see you."

Clarissa twisted toward the captain.

"Please." He gestured. "I hope she's feeling better."

She padded across the floorboards and opened a door at the back of the room. She slipped inside the chamber and closed the door behind her.

Harriet sat on a sofa, her cheek resting on the cushion. Something was wrong.

Clarissa dashed to her sister's side and knelt. "Harriet? What is it?"

Harriet turned a cheerless face to hers. "He seems familiar."

Clarissa grew cold. "You don't say that with merriment."

Harriet rolled away. "But I've never actually chanced upon him sooner than today."

"You haven't?"

"No. I'm sure of it."

Worry coiled through Clarissa's gut. "What is amiss? Do you sense the captain is not as he appears?"

"Something…" She turned back. "Use caution, Clarissa. Something *is* wrong." Harriet gave her fingers a squeeze. "I see you're falling in love with him."

If Harriet were right vis-à-vis her suspicions… "He respects my education. How rare that trait is in a gentleman. And for him to feed that quality in me is wonderful. He's a singular treasure, sister."

"Go on. Do not linger here."

"But you're…"

"I need a little rest. It's no more than that."

Clarissa returned to her brother and the captain.

Gilbert looked at her in question.

"She's only a little tired."

He nodded.

"That is good to hear." The captain smiled.

She took her seat while Gilbert reached for a pack of cards.

"Miss Hale, I would enjoy sweeping you across a ballroom floor as they do in a foreign country. You would be so beautiful floating across the room in my arms." His bold words took her by surprise.

She blinked, mesmerized. "That's lovely." She glanced at Gilbert, suddenly embarrassed, remembering he was there.

Gilbert was grinning.

"I'm afraid such sentiments are a weakness of mine," the captain said.

"I consider them to be of great merit."

"My brother thinks I'm a fool because of my tendencies," Captain Amberley said.

"Your brother could not win my affections." It fell from her lips.

She set her cards on her lap and reached for her teacup as he bent for his. Their fingertips made contact, sending tingles through her.

A powerful jolt flooded her senses. *I belong with you.* His nearness seared a path of joy through her spirit.

"Whose deal?" Gilbert asked.

~ * ~

After the captain left, Gilbert leaned on his cane, brandishing a smug smile.

"Gilbert, tell me why you are grinning."

He shrugged.

"Brother, tell me." She balled her fists on her hips.

"I imagine you and the captain will be happy should this continue. It will develop into a love match."

She touched her chest. "Yes."

"He said the two of you are compatible, and he is delighted."

"He made my heart race. I have never been affected so."

"Oh?" Gilbert asked with a smirk. "More than that cad you once were tied to?"

"Much more."

He tipped his head in approval.

~ * ~

The captain came by the shop daily and made expensive purchases. He recommended it to his friends. Gilbert was happy to see him whenever he walked through the door. Often, during slow business times, he sometimes, but more often Clarissa, pulled up a stool and carried on conversations across the counter. Sometimes Captain Amberley and Clarissa discussed art. Sometimes horses, literature, antiques, other countries, or any number of things. When she asked him an even mildly personal question, she switched to French, such as inquiring about his brother.

One such day Gilbert turned from the shelf of books he was rearranging. "That French word means *brother*."

"Indeed," Clarissa said, then faced the captain.

"My brother..." he hesitated.

"Is this not a subject you care to discuss?"

He glanced down briefly. "It is of no consequence."

"Is he much younger than you?"

"No, only a couple of years."

"Does he share common traits with you?"

"He resembles me in appearance, as you have seen, but that is all. We are otherwise completely different."

"How unusual. Gilbert and I are alike in temperament. How are you two different?"

He cleared his throat. "Miss Hale, it is difficult for me to describe to a lady I respect."

She gaped then recovered herself. "Is he...so bad?"

"I will say only he is careless and does not often think of the future, his or anyone else's."

"Would you say he resembles the author Lord Byron in temperament?"

The captain chuckled. "A man notorious for his passionate affairs with women, but..."

"Please," she said in French still. "I will take no offense. My brother does not comprehend French as his wife does and will not understand. Tell me."

"My brother does not particularly esteem women, not the way I esteem you. He would never be interested in discussing the things I regularly discuss with you."

"Oh? Captain, as you have gathered by now, part of the reason I am so unusual to you is that I have a prodigious imagination."

"You do, and I admire that."

"Thank you." She played absentmindedly with a ribbon on her glove. "Match it, and paint a picture for me, if you will."

His smile grew wide. "I enjoy a challenge. All right. If women went to universities with men, and we were two students, we would be chatting in the library about world events now. If Ewan rendezvoused with a woman there, she would end up..." he straightened his cravat, "not in a library, and they would not be engaged in intelligent conversation."

She looked down a moment.

He sighed happily. "Did I meet your challenge, Miss Hale?"

"Yes," she said, dreamily. *You respect me and my oddness.*

Gilbert turned to them. "If you two are done conversing in French, I will interrupt a moment. I must do inventory behind the curtain, mere feet away. Sister, call me up front if I am needed."

"Certainly." She glanced at him as he disappeared behind the curtain.

Suddenly, the door to the shop opened. A man in rags walked in, bringing in the cold air. Clarissa greeted him with a smile and approached him. The captain watched with avid interest. Did he think such a man would offend Clarissa?

"Mr. Ruthers, how do you fare today?"

"Ah, Miss Hale, it's a bit cold. I needed sunshine, so I made my way to your fine family establishment."

"You flatter me, sir. Come, sit."

She dragged over a stool for him, by her main countertop, and introduced the two men.

The captain tipped his hat. "How long have you known Miss Hale?"

"A couple of years now. An angel she is."

"Good sirs, let me retrieve a little tea." She disappeared a moment in the back and returned with a tea service for three. The captain waited as she poured the steaming beige liquid into three delicate china cups. A steamy flowery scent ascended. The captain would have known she had heated water in the little fireplace, had a kettle on the fire already. Mr. Ruthers was rubbing his dirty palms together, creating a scratching friction sound against the calluses.

"Here sir, this will warm you up. Tell me news of your life," she said.

The captain sipped the tea as Clarissa's homeless acquaintance chatted with her about life in the gutter, life in his neighborhood, which vendor cheated whom or which boy unearthed lodgings for the week or who came across a shilling accidentally and shared it with the others. A shopkeeper threw out a perfectly good blanket and now it warmed a family of three on the streets. Clarissa went to the back again for bread. She ripped off a sizable chunk and gave it to Mr. Ruthers. She offered some to the captain, but he declined it. After a cheerful conversation, Clarissa gave Mr. Ruthers a stern look.

"What is that for, Miss Hale?"

"I now require payment for the food and drink, sir."

The captain's brows rose. Mr. Ruthers turned his pockets inside out, dispelling lint. "I'm afraid I have nothing in my pockets, Miss."

The captain reached for his coin bag. Clarissa's slippered feet made a soft padding sound as she crossed the polished wood floor of the room. The shop door made a click as she locked it. She returned, and the captain squinted in curiosity as Mr. Ruthers was beaming on his seat.

Clarissa went behind the counter and reached for two small swords. "I knew I'd have a use for these. Then a lesson, kind sir!"

Mr. Ruthers laughed. "I used to have a school in Paris in my youth."

He reached for the sword, stood, and bowed to Clarissa. She did the same.

"Yes, previous to the war. Then you closed shop and returned home. Unfortunately, you did not prosper in this and have not been able to find other work."

"Miss Hale, you make me feel twenty again, strong, useful, and talented. Thank you for allowing me to practice my passion."

"I'm not very good, but here it goes anyway. On guard!"

The captain's eyes were wide as they sparred, amusement apparent on his face. She was rather awful at the art and knew it. After a while, the two stopped and bowed to each other. Clarissa took the sword from him and gave him another crusty loaf of bread and a large chunk of pale cheese, along with an apple the color of Christmas ribbons.

The captain reached into his bag and retrieved several coins. He gave them to Mr. Ruthers.

"Sir, come by my estate. I need a new groomsman in my stable. Would you be interested? Teach my stable boys to use a sword too. I'd pay you extra for that."

"Really?"

"Really."

"Thank you, sir."

The captain gave the man his address, and after Mr. Ruthers left happy, Captain Amberley gave Clarissa a penetrating look.

"I hope you don't think I'm mad now, sir, for my sword playing."

"No. I find you caring and good, and surprising. How else will you surprise me, Miss Hale?"

She felt herself flush in the suddenly overly-warm room. She looked behind her as if someone had stoked the fire in the back and it was now blazing.

"I find myself affected in your presence. Enchanted," he nearly whispered.

"I'm...different. My books have fired my imagination to a great degree."

One brow rose over curious green eyes. "And?"

She remained silent.

"On my honor, you can tell me."

"Well, you see, my aunt married a gypsy, and as a child, I would visit them. My exposure to my uncle's culture, I suppose, is what contributed to my..." She turned her attention to the wooden floor. "Differentness."

"Miss Hale."

She looked up, at him.

"I sense...shame? There is no reason for that. Recall I am well-traveled. I respect other cultures greatly, as...different as they may be from ours, and as much as I esteem our great country. Your unusual qualities—"

"Unusual qualities?"

"Maybe this will make you understand." He leaned forward, contemplating her with love. As their fingers made contact, two women entered the shop.

Clarissa sprang to her feet. The captain fiddled with his packages on the counter.

"Will there be anything else, sir?" she said to him.

"No, Miss, thank you. I will be back because I am working on particular collections, and your shop has quality items."

"At good prices, sir, but I will never give out the secret of my sources."

"Miss, charge me triple what your competitors would, and I would still come here."

"Why?" she teased.

The two women were casually taking in the shop's items.

"Because I respect your advice. You said you shall have a certain item in by tomorrow?"

"Yes," Clarissa said.

"Then tomorrow. Good day."

"Good day."

He tipped his head then left the shop, smiling.

Please come back, for the rest of my life.

~ * ~

The next day, Gilbert went up to his rooms early. Clarissa closed the shop door, her shoulders slumped. The captain had not arrived. As soon as she ran into Gilbert in the corridor above, he asked why she was so glum. She would not say, so he suggested a walk, saying the shining sun would make the snow sparkle like diamonds and cheer her. They left through the tinkling door of the shop.

The snow crunched under their feet as they passed by several fashionable boutiques. They walked by a window where colorful silks and muslins hung in folds in order to be admired, organized in patterns to appeal to the senses. Clarissa barely noticed. In her mind she saw him, the tall, well-built naval officer who captivated her. She stopped walking, whispering his name.

Gilbert regarded her. "Clarissa?"

She grabbed his arm and urged him forward. Shouts rushed their feet forward. A crowd had gathered. She and Gilbert stopped and gaped. In the middle of the group, the captain spoke firmly to a man dressed in the fashion of the middling classes in his suitable attire. A diminutive third man cowered nearby.

"It is utterly inexcusable to treat someone that way!" the captain said.

His opponent spit out, "He calls himself an American! Of course I spit on him, the trash! You served for England's glory. How could you defend this man?"

"Easily! He did nothing to merit your abuse!" He shoved a finger toward him.

"Traitor!"

The captain inclined toward him ominously and spoke with ice. "I would die for the crown. I am a loyal servant of England. Do not forget that! Ever!"

Several lingering men agreed. "Hero!" someone called out, looking at him.

"But you shield the American! Our enemy!"

"He's defended England numerous times!" a shout came from among the onlookers.

The captain thanked the man then looked at his accuser. "He is no such thing! In case you haven't heard, the war is over. We lost. Decades ago. Time to congratulate them on becoming an independent nation, like gentlemen would, and move on!"

"But relations are troubled with the Yankees now."

"True. Let us hope nothing becomes of it. It is not like they have attacked England. It is not as if they have conducted themselves as

Napoleon has! I've seen the difference. More than thirty years ago, they craved independence. Napoleon takes independence from millions, as he marches across Europe, mad for power. Besides, I was born after the War for Independence ended. I hold no resentment towards the Americans. They are our brothers! We may have trouble brewing now, but brothers are expected to disagree, not *kill* each other."

Clarissa smiled. The captain helped the American to stand up straight, and the man thanked him.

The captain turned and noticed Clarissa. "Excuse me." He went to her as the crowd stared. He bowed and looked at her intently.

Clarissa and the captain walked along the row of shops with Gilbert, Clarissa's official escort, at a respectable distance behind them.

~ * ~

Gilbert gave Clarissa a cup of tea. "You should see the portrait Harriet is painting in our rooms."

"I'm sure it's a wonder," Clarissa said, sitting on her couch, near her brother in her own rooms. Harriet had had an interesting conversation with her earlier, reminding her of the night the captain had first come for tea.

"He fancies you most well."

She gave Gilbert a sad smile. "But I'm afraid."

His brow creased. "Whatever for?"

"On the night they were introduced, Harriet harbored a strange sensation that something was amiss."

Gilbert set his tea down. "She is usually correct. Should I tell the captain not to call on you again?" His voice wavered as if he were unsure, confused.

"No!" She fidgeted with the tea service.

"I see you're distressed."

"I have to see this out. I'm many things, Gilbert, but I am not a coward."

"Do you believe the situation requires courage? Is there something you're not telling me?"

"You're aware of the secret Harriet refuses to tell us?"

"Yeees?" he drew out.

"I think the captain is somehow in some way connected."

"What?" he snapped. "Harriet disappeared for months. Remember she came back miserable." His hands curled into fists on his lap.

"I don't think Captain Amberley is directly involved, but I sense if I see this through, we'll find answers."

"See this through? Not if it puts my sister in danger, we won't. Excuse me a moment."

He strode across the room, then the narrow corridor and to his and Harriet's rooms, coming out moments later, huffing. "Harriet believes something is definitely amiss. She can't recall, but she supposes she may have seen him somewhere, and not in the best of situations. I'm sending a note to Captain Amberley and telling him to stay away."

"You can't!"

"He troubled my wife, and now you say these things to me! I'll get my answers from Harriet eventually, and then I'll take action. I don't need you in the line of fire."

"No, I think I love him." She gripped his wrist.

"I'm sorry. It's over. I'm your guardian and, on this I must insist."

"In less than a year, I will be one and twenty."

He scowled. "Are you implying you wish to...defy me and break away from our family? Your inheritance, your part of the family shop?"

"No," she uttered through a tight throat.

He put a finger under her chin. "Good. It's not what Father would have wanted. You'd break Mother's heart."

"Oh!" She spun away from him, assailed with bitterness.

Three

Duncan sat in his study, a dark room filled with heavy wooden furniture and portraits of thoroughbred horses. Sipping his brandy, he crossed his booted feet under a massive oak desk, and glanced at his younger brother.

Ewan often gave him cause for concern with his womanizing ways, but Duncan rested easily now. He might safely discuss Clarissa, for they were proceeding with a formal courtship.

"There's something different about you, brother, as of late." Ewan dragged Duncan from his reverie. "You don't brood much anymore. You were so serious and responsible in the past, but lately you're an inhalation of fresh air. I'm greatly amused. What has happened to cause this change?"

"Fate has brought me to the woman I mean to spend my life with."

"Who?"

"A woman so beautiful I can barely comprehend my good fortune."

Ewan shifted in his leather chair. "You are jesting?"

"No."

"Have you stumbled upon the perfect heiress? Is that why you waste no time?" He took a sip from his own glass.

Duncan thought of her. *I hope to give Clarissa a happy life. She is a jewel. If I don't act fast, another man may sweep her away.*

"You've met her, Ewan."

His brother raised an eyebrow. "Oh?"

"The lovely lady who with her brother required assistance the night of our gathering."

"What? But she's...a...a shopkeeper!" Ewan rubbed his forehead. "Why not just bed her?"

"I would never treat her with such disrespect."

"This is absurd. You cannot chain yourself to a shopkeeper." He hit his armrest with a fist. "Our father worked too hard to raise us in rank." Leaning back in his chair, he curled his lip derisively. "Seduce her. I would. Have scores of mistresses."

"Have another mistress? I would be dallying with less of a woman. I'm done with that. Ewan, she is divine." He rested his forearm on his knee.

"If she were not so beautiful, would you be tying yourself to her in this way?"

Duncan pondered what he was going to say. "I admit it was her appearance that compelled me to pursue her in the first place."

"Ah, so I have my answer."

That damn smirk. Unbecoming, my brother.

"No, you do not." Duncan considered him. "Of course that was what started it all, but I have spoken with her at length. We are compatible, and it will be a good match. I have been with other beautiful women without falling in love or longing for marriage. I have been taken with a woman previously, when I was younger. Felicia was not what you would consider a great beauty. I became acquainted with her when my crew took leave on an island."

"You never told me."

"No. I spent a great deal of time with her. She nursed me after I was injured from a battle with the French. My feelings for her grew. They were based on respect and companionship more than physical attraction."

"Did you love her anyway?" Ewan's voice revealed surprise.

"I felt the beginnings of that, then one day was informed she had run off and married a doctor. I was shocked and would not fall so easily the next time, happy it had happened before I could fully feel love and utter those words. I vowed to myself I would never so easily prepare to say them again."

"And?"

"When I found myself in the middle of the ocean again, it occurred to me I couldn't really blame Felicia. I was nowhere near ready to retire from the Navy and remain on land to raise a family, not even for her, and she knew that. I was not a captain yet and had limited choices."

"Your new woman..." Ewan dropped off.

"I did not speak of her earlier because I did not wish for your interference. Now it's safe for you to be informed."

Ewan glared at him.

"I would have left the Navy for her, searched for a way. If not, I would have brought her with me. Captain's privileges."

"But why *her*? I passed ten beauties on my way to the club."

"Why do you not want me to marry?"

"I don't fancy you marrying *her*, and I don't believe in love. She's using you for your money. Marry someone who will make you even wealthier, a lady accustomed to polite society. But I suppose you'll need an heir someday. If not, all will pass to me."

"If you marry, I'll settle some land on you on which you can raise a family."

Ewan scoffed. "A wife? No, thank you. I'll enjoy the money my allowance brings and the women I fancy without having to come home to the same one daily."

"Love has its charms," Duncan said.

"Haven't others fallen for *you*?"

He took a drink. "Yes, a few."

"You took them to your bed without caring for them?"

"I cared for them."

"I'm confused."

"Miss Hale is most unusual. I must marry her."

"So, you bedded the ones you did not have to have, and refuse to do so with the woman you must have. Interesting."

Duncan grinned. "I will be with her every day for the rest of my life."

"You haven't answered my question."

"Even if she were not so attractive, I would still think her a wonderful woman. I would crave her company and look forward to being in her presence."

Ewan snapped his fingers. "But she's not plain."

"No. Stop giving me that look, man. If my Clarissa were not so fetching, I would still want to pull her into my arms. I could never get my fill of that woman."

"What do you admire most in her?"

"So many things...her interesting mind—"

"That's not what I mean."

Duncan studied him.

"Tell me what I yearn to hear." Ewan downed his drink.

"She's elegant, graceful, and charming, not to mention clever."

"Huh." Ewan crossed an ankle over his knee. "Fascinating. You've never spoken of a woman this way."

"Remember she—if all goes well—is my future wife. Do not harbor any foolish ideas when you next see her. I desire her for more than her appearance. You would only tolerate her unusual ambitions until you tired of her in bed. I will never tire of such an interesting, stimulating woman. It's my goal to lead a simple life with the woman I love."

Ewan laughed, but a suspicious glint danced in his eyes. "Brooding again, Duncan. You're humorless. How could a woman put up with you for a lifetime? You don't laugh often. She'd be bored to tears. You've been cheerful lately, but it's due to the newness of the situation, I believe. Give it a few months, and you'll be back to your old self."

"Aren't you the clever one?"

"Let's not forget fortunate as well. I usually have my way."

"She and I can discuss numerous things with intelligence." Duncan glanced down.

"How exciting."

Duncan sipped the last of his drink. "Congratulate me. She's the perfect woman for me. And we will have beautiful, intelligent children. I rather like the thought of that. I appreciate Miss Hale. She may be sweet and sensitive, but she has purpose in life, dreams and goals. I will never take the hope of that from her. I respect it and will feed her ambitions."

The smirk showed itself again. "She has purpose? Do you speak of religion?"

"No, her family shop. She and her brother run it exceptionally well."

Ewan stood, poured himself another drink, and then dropped into his chair. "Surely you won't allow her to participate in commerce if she accepts your proposal." He took a gulp of his brandy.

"Yes, I will. When I saw a similar look in a midshipman, I nurtured the ambition. Why would I crush it in a woman for whom I harbor such strong feelings? We will have a happy home."

"You are mad." He shrugged. "And will be ostracized for having a working wife."

"A small price to pay to win and keep her devotion."

"Don't marry Miss Hale," Ewan ordered. "I won't let you. Marriage to her will disgrace our family."

Duncan saw red. "And how do you propose to stop me?"

Ewan sneered with the malice he had possessed since they were boys. He took the last of his brandy in one swallow.

"Get out of here," Duncan thundered. "Out!"

"Bossy..."

~ * ~

Ewan fumed, pondering Miss Hale as he strolled down Oxford Street. "We're gentry now. He must marry an heiress. Besides, she's too beautiful. I want her," he muttered, and silently congratulated himself on his prowess. Having paid a publisher a hefty sum to do his bidding and spoken to Miss Donovan, Duncan's former mistress, as well, he might now return home.

~ * ~

Clarissa stared down at the note by their main counter.

Gilbert peered over her shoulder. "What is that?"

"Oh, Mr. Jensen down the road has offered an excellent bargain on books, but only today. I'm to meet him at once. Look out for the shop?"

"By all means. Hurry back. I worry when you're out on your own."

She reached for her jacket. "I won't be long."

"Are you sure you would not prefer to have me close the shop and accompany you, or go upstairs and ask Harriet to go with you? Let's hope this is the day she ventures out of our rooms."

"I'll be fine." She dashed out of the door. Thoughts of the captain warmed her as she strolled past window shops. She'd think of a way to bring Gilbert around.

In Mr. Jensen's shop, near the door, he greeted her with a slight bow. "Miss Hale? How do you do?"

"I am well, sir. And you?"

"Very well, Miss."

Clarissa glanced around, admiring his stock of books.

"Excuse me." An attractive blonde woman turned her attention from the book she had been considering and faced Clarissa.

Clarissa inhaled sharply, recognizing her.

"Miss Hale? It's me, Elizabeth Donovan, Captain Amberley's... well, he and I were somewhat attached..." her voice trailed off.

Mr. Jensen nodded, his features politely expressionless. "Excuse me." He walked across his shop and spoke with a woman glancing around as if she had never been there.

Clarissa considered Miss Donovan. "Yes. I remember seeing you the day I made the acquaintance of the captain, at his home."

Miss Donovan took a step near Clarissa. "Are you really thinking of marrying him?"

"I...how are you aware of this?"

"He told me about you."

The hair rose at Clarissa's nape. "Excuse me." She walked toward Mr. Jensen's counter.

Miss Donovan followed her. Clarissa cringed and walked across the shop to peruse a row of books. Again, the annoying lady pursued her. Two ladies on the other side of the room were involved in their own conversation, and Mr. Jensen was showing a lady a small volume.

"Miss Hale, for your own good, I must tell you Duncan and I walked out for over a year, and there are still unresolved matters with us. Love."

Clarissa nearly missed the last, softly spoken word. She did not move. *This is suspicious. You are a former mistress. Perchance you hunger for revenge because he ended it?* She lifted her chin.

"You don't believe me? Would you rather discover the truth after the marriage?"

"What?"

"Think of the regrets you'd have. He's deceiving you. Do you wish to take the chance I'm lying to you?"

Harriet was suspicious of him, saying something wasn't right. No, no. No.

She turned and hurried out without what she had come for. Once on the street, she hastened her steps, the tears running down her face unheeded.

Why, when I finally find another man whom I can love, who respects me, can I not have him and be happy? Her salty tears hitting her lips, she swiped them away.

When she arrived at the Hale Emporium, Duncan was approaching the front door, his face glowing with happiness. He was near his carriage, snow dusting his hat and greatcoat like crystal stars twinkling against a black sky.

So, Gilbert hasn't seen you yet.

He bowed outside the door. "Good day, Miss Hale."

Her chest tightened with sadness. "Good day." She kept her distance and didn't look directly at him. She peered into the shop window.

From the reflection in the glass, she saw his lips curve down. "Miss Hale, what has happened?" His voice was so soft, she barely perceived it.

A well-dressed woman and her maid strolled by. They stopped in front of the Hale shop and glanced inside. Clarissa waited to see if they would go inside and pretended not to notice the captain. The ladies turned and continued walking.

Clarissa tossed Duncan the briefest of looks. She didn't care for a scene with Gilbert, although her throat constricted with tears as she thought of the captain and Miss Donovan. Clarissa would end this now...and be frequented with his memory.

Why must I love you?

"Though I may not be of the same sphere as you, I have dignity. I will not continue this liaison under these circumstances," she said in soft tones she knew only he'd hear.

He took a step closer. "Miss Hale, to what are you referring?"

She shuddered, mortified. "Your connection with Miss Donovan."

He exhaled sharply. "It is finished between us. You have nothing to fear."

This was crushing, but she dug up her courage. "Not according to her. She seems to be under the impression you two are still...in love."

"That's absurd. And we never were *in love*."

A ripple of anger at his deceit rushed her. "I saw her! She told me herself."

He clenched his jaw. "It was not meant to be. I have broken my ties with her and would not pursue an inappropriate relationship once engaged to be married or afterward."

"I would *never* marry a man who does."

A gray-haired couple wandered by, glancing at them. Duncan turned away, as if he were a stranger to Clarissa. The couple continued along.

Duncan faced Clarissa again, with tenderness in his tone. "Miss Hale, listen to me. I promise you, I will be true."

If only.

"And I would like to be married soon," he said.

Doubts trickled through her, drawing a shiver. Her previous fiancé had betrayed her. She watched the captain as her emotions created havoc in her mind. "Captain Amberley—"

"Duncan."

When two men happened by, she glimpsed around the road as if searching for someone. The strangers passed, and she fidgeted with her cuffs. "As a girl of eighteen, I nearly rushed into marriage. I won't do that again. I must be sure—" *And find a way to convince Gilbert...*

He spoke under his breath, his attention directed at his carriage, not her, so passersby couldn't see they were in conversation with each other. "About what? My integrity? I vow to you, I will not desert you for Miss Donovan or any other woman. Once you are mine, I will *treasure* you."

She dared a glance his way. *You speak the truth. Oh, you speak the truth.* A smile of happy relief spread across her face.

He turned to her. She nodded, and a smile came to his lips. Two women left the shop, followed by Gilbert. The ladies continued down the street. Clarissa looked at her brother's narrowed brow and ordered the shakiness in her limbs to stop. She and the captain stepped back.

"Good day, Mr. Hale." Captain Amberley turned to her. "Miss Hale, I came to invite you to a performance at Covent Garden."

"Captain, how long have you been out here? I was engaged with customers."

"Mere moments."

"I'd prefer to escort my sister until she has a husband."

He glanced at Gilbert. "Of course. Tonight. Will you join me in my box?"

"We'll be there but separately. I was planning on purchasing tickets as a surprise for Clarissa."

Her brows lifted at the unexpected news.

"Would you join me at intermission?"

Clarissa's breath suspended. What would Gilbert say?

"No, and you will not call on my sister again."

Her chest tightened. *What could I expect?*

"What are you saying?"

"It's finished." Gilbert glanced at people passing on the street and gestured for Duncan and Clarissa to follow him inside the shop. "Come inside. We're clear for the moment," he said with cool anger.

"I don't understand!" the captain expressed.

"I don't approve. What else is there to say?"

"Mr. Hale, what have I done?" The captain tugged on his cravat.

"I owe you no explanation."

What am I going to do?

"Is this regarding Miss Donovan? Has she spoken with you as well?"

He studied the captain under a narrowed brow. "As a matter of fact, yes. She was in the shop."

"Mr. Hale, as a gentleman, I ask you to reconsider your position. I have nothing but the best intentions regarding Clarissa. I do not understand why Miss Donovan would do this."

Clarissa grabbed Gilbert's arm, pleading with him. *Please, brother.*

Gilbert turned to the captain. "We shall see. You will have to prove yourself. We'll continue this conversation later."

Hope.

"Thank you." Duncan bowed to Clarissa and left.

Gilbert turned to her. "I want you to be happy." He tapped her arm. "And it is a bit suspicious about Miss Donovan."

I love you, Gilbert, and I love Duncan.

~ * ~

Clarissa and Gilbert waited for the performance to begin. She scanned the theater, up at the boxes near the front. Well-dressed people chatted, but Duncan wasn't among them.

"I wonder where he is." She glanced at her brother. Recognition painted Gilbert's features, and she trailed the direction of his gaze.

Across the way, Captain Amberley sustained the look.

"You wish to see him, sister. Come, we must gather more information. I honestly do not sense the bad things Harriet spoke of, but I will be on guard. However, I will give him a chance because you seem determined about this."

"I am."

They proceeded in the captain's direction.

He greeted them with a bow. "Good evening, Miss Hale, Mr. Hale. How do you do?"

"Well, and you?" Clarissa asked.

"Not too bad." He turned to Gilbert. "And you?"

"Well enough."

They chatted for a few minutes in an open area as people walked by. Clarissa brought up a humorous book she had recently read, and the captain laughed lightly. When Gilbert did as well, Clarissa studied them, reveling in the happy moment.

"Well, I suppose we'd better take our seats."

"Yes, Captain." Gilbert extended his arm to Clarissa, and she took it.

At intermission, she excused herself to go to a retiring room. Once there, she noticed Miss Donovan crying.

Clarissa approached and reached out but drew back. "Miss Donovan."

"Why is he doing this? We still love each other."

Clarissa inhaled sharply. "I..." She dashed out of the room.

Gilbert turned and saw Clarissa dabbing at her wet cheeks, so he bound to his feet. "Clarissa?"

"She was here, Gilbert, crying. Oh!"

"We're going home. I have my answers."

"Please," she said. "I need air."

He escorted her out. The captain called to them from the lobby, a few feet away. "Mr. Hale, Miss Hale."

Gilbert waved him away. "Leave us be. We do not wish to converse with you."

"But—"

"Good evening, Captain. Never call on my sister again."

People in the near vicinity stopped talking and stared at her and Gilbert. Clarissa made out the word Cits, and swallowed hard, embarrassed.

"Come, Clarissa." Gilbert's features strained with rage.

~ * ~

The captain burst into her empty shop the next morning as they opened. Clarissa ran to the back while Gilbert took a step in his direction.

There's going to be an ugly scene. She gripped the edge of the curtain that divided the shop from the rear of the building.

"Didn't I make myself clear? Leave my sister alone."

"I cannot. I want her as my wife."

"You'd back down as a gentleman would if we weren't lowly shopkeepers... or perhaps you're not a gentleman."

"I beg you, forgive my behavior."

Heartbroken and trembling, Clarissa listened. He had never acted in this manner, she knew.

The clink of Gilbert's walking stick rattled across the floorboards as he strode to Duncan. "Leave, and never return. The courtship is done."

"Miss Hale," Duncan shouted, stretching to look past Gilbert. "Please, Miss Hale, hear me."

His voice cut through her with tenderness. She released the curtain and would give him a chance to explain.

"Get out," Gilbert repeated.

"I beg you to hear me out."

"Out." Gilbert thrust his finger toward the door.

"Wait." *I must give you the benefit of a doubt. If I don't, I'll forever regret it.*

"No, Clarissa, I—"

"Please." She strode past Gilbert to Captain Amberley.

"What have you to say, Captain? I will hear you."

A pained expression stressed his features. "Miss Hale, you are important to me. Help me to understand what has happened. I'm at a loss." He spoke with sadness and sincerity.

"Miss Donovan approached me last night, crying of your ill-treatment of her."

"She has ulterior motives."

"And why am I to suppose that? I stumbled upon her, not the other way around."

"Believe me for love's sake, Miss Hale. I go there often. Imaginably she thought to find us there together, and went in search of an opportunity. I wonder what she requires of me."

"She said *you* told her news of us."

"My brother. Yes, it had to be Ewan."

I love you, Duncan. Yes, I believe you, against my own vision, for the sake of those feelings.

"Why are you doing this to my sister? You mean to ruin her!"

"Mr. Hale, I adore your sister. I have no dishonorable intentions."

"Miss Donovan says differently."

"Miss Donovan is a bitter woman."

Her fingertips flew to her lips. *Duncan?*

The captain turned to her. "What will it take to make you believe?"

"Captain…"

"Believe me."

She glanced at Gilbert.

"She will not have my blessing whilst I harbor such serious doubts about you."

"I am unhappy to hear that."

"And, I have it from other sources you might not be what you seem."

He referred to Harriet's apprehensions.

"I'm sure I do not grasp what you mean. A tragic mistake has been made. I promise on my honor as a captain and a gentleman, sir," he said gravely. "Have me investigated, and you will discover I speak the truth." He tipped his hat and dashed out of the shop.

A soft sob fell from Clarissa's lips. Would Gilbert do everything in his power to stop the marriage? Would she lose someone she cared for so much? Would she have to choose between him and Duncan?

Gilbert stroked her arm. "Hush, there."

"I love him."

He withdrew an embroidered cloth from his pocket and wiped her tears. "I have an idea."

A spark of hope awoke in her.

Four

"What are we doing here, Gilbert?" Clarissa sat on a stool behind the curtain separating Mrs. Lankston's workshop from her showroom.

The hour was late, half past closing. A single lantern near the front dimly lit the hat-filled showroom.

"Clarissa, Mrs. Lankston is so kind to agree to help out. Our delightful milliner sent a note to the captain in which she explained you wished to meet him here in private."

"I don't understand, Gilbert."

"I also had a note sent to Miss Donovan. I paid someone to find her. The captain supposedly signed the note. Actually it was I. The note said to meet him here, alone, and that the proprietor wishes to present her with a costly gift he paid for in advance to win back her affections."

"What are you doing?"

"Listen through the curtain. You'll receive the answers you long for."

"Gilbert, I believe him. This isn't necessary."

"And good news. You remember I told you I'd have him investigated."

"Yes?"

"His references came back in his favor."

"I knew they would!"

"And Harriet says she might have been mistaken."

"Yes."

"Now, if only we can assure ourselves of his fidelity, because I recognize how important of an issue that is to you."

"What am I—"

"Shh!"

The bell tinkled, signaling someone being let into the dark hat shop.

"Good evening, Captain Amberley." Mrs. Lankston greeted the fine-looking visitor.

"Good evening, madam."

Clarissa's stomach fluttered.

"Where is Miss Hale? She agreed to meet me here." Eagerness lightened the captain's tutored voice.

Right here, Duncan. I'm right here. Prove yourself for me.

"Yes. She wishes to meet you here because her brother is suspicious of you."

"I must speak with Miss Hale."

"I see. Excuse me. Well, she's not here, but wait. I must go above stairs for a moment." Mrs. Lankston walked to the rear of the shop and slipped behind the curtain, standing in darkness behind Clarissa.

Gilbert gripped Clarissa's shoulder in a show of support. The shop door opened.

"Duncan," Miss Donovan uttered.

Your voice saddens me, Miss Donovan. If only I never had to hear it again. Duncan, please, send her away forever. Clarissa inched toward the curtain.

"What are you doing here?"

You sound astonished to find her here and not happy. Good.

"I...I don't understand!" Miss Donovan's fingers fluttered to her throat.

"Why are you doing this to me?"

You sound sad, Duncan, and vexed. I long for you to put your arms around me. I'll bring you peace.

"We shared such a passionate love."

"It wasn't love, and you know it!"

Clarissa's fingertips came to her lips. The suspense gripped her.

"Oh, Duncan!" Miss Donovan cried.

"I did care for you, but..."

"Please, reconsider."

No, Duncan. She'll bring you uncertainty.

"You knew from the beginning what we were. I never gave you false impressions."

Oh thank goodness. You didn't do her wrong. She had false hopes she created herself.

"But I thought to change your mind."

"I'm going to marry Miss Hale." His posture stiffened.

Because you love me, or you might with time. You respect me more than you do her.

"Are you determined?"

"Yes!"

Clarissa sat up straighter, stiffening her spine in surprise at the level of his irritation.

"Why not me?"

"She has won me over."

Clarissa smiled, and Gilbert tapped her shoulder.

"Well then..." she hesitated. "Perhaps—"

"Perhaps what?"

"You can set me up."

"What we had is finished. Keep out of my life. Do you understand me? I intend to be a faithful husband to Clarissa. Do not harbor any further notions about you and me."

I love you, Duncan.

"You cannot mean that!"

"I do, Miss Donovan."

Miss Donovan's quick footsteps thudded on the floorboards, and the door slammed shut. Mrs. Lankston made her way to Duncan.

"Where is Miss Hale?" He looked out the window.

"Go to her shop on the morrow at closing time. I'm sure she will see you."

"Thank you, madam." He turned and left.

~ * ~

Duncan entered the Hale Emporium, empty at this time except for Clarissa. Instant tears came to Clarissa's eyes. Mr. Hale was not around.

Duncan hesitated. "I'm no longer involved with Miss Donovan, I promise you."

"I believe you. I think I always did." A half-smile curved her lips.

Surprise made his heart skip a beat. "You did?"

"Yes."

"And..." *Tell me more, my sweet Clarissa.*

"What is it?"

How are you going to react to what I'm preparing to say? I pray I will not lose you. "Well, the nature of my feelings dictate, I have to ask, but understand I do so with reserve."

She took a step closer. "Yes?"

You're looking at me with love. I'm so delighted. "Forgive me. Your brother is your guardian, and you're not...one and twenty yet? Almost?"

"I will be in less than a year."

I must do this. He reached for her. "I realize you love and respect him. But might you..."

"You are hesitant." Her brow rose. "Are you asking me to defy him?"

My intelligent dear. His feet garnered his attention briefly. Mild shame heated his nape. "Remember you will not have to depend on him financially, sweetheart." His natural courage, honed on a ship, shot through him. "He loves you. He'll forgive you, and I'll be such a good husband to you that he'll come around."

Her lips curved downward. "Our father put it in his will that if Gilbert didn't approve of my marriage, I would be cut off from the shop completely. I cannot abide the thought of that."

Oh, no. "I see." *Please sacrifice that for me. I'll make it up to you. Think.* Inspiration came to him. "I will buy you a shop of your own."

"What? You would allow me to continue my work," she muttered, "but I knew that." Her shoulders took a dive. "No. My family shop is important to me."

His heart constricted. "My love—"

"My brother has changed his mind. He will give his blessing."

Did I hear you right? "And you? Do you wish to wed me?"

"Yes."

"You've thought this out. You care for me."

"Yes."

"Why didn't you meet me last night at the milliner's?"

"I'll tell you someday. Not today, Captain."

"Call me *Duncan*."

"Duncan."

The way you say my name… Images of kissing her with passion flooded his mind. "You'll marry me as soon as possible?"

"Yes."

He kissed her cheek.

~ * ~

The small church glowed with candles. White flowers in vases added grace to the elegant ceremony. Clarissa stared at her love as the reverend spoke sacred words. Duncan slid a gold ring onto her finger with veneration. Tears of joy thickened her throat.

Once the reverend announced they were husband and wife, Clarissa looked at the small gathering of their smiling friends. Her brother-in-law, Ewan, glared. Trepidation traced up her spine.

He hates me.

During the wedding breakfast at the Amberley estate, Duncan spoke with cheer to their guests. He turned to Gilbert first, though, and expressed his regrets because Harriet was ill in bed.

"Thank you, and now I regret I must return home to attend to her," Gilbert said. "She anxiously awaits hearing news of the wedding."

"I'm disappointed Harriet wasn't here," Clarissa whispered, and embraced Gilbert. "Give her my love."

"I will." Gilbert kissed Clarissa's cheek. "I love you."

"I love you too."

Gilbert walked outside to his borrowed coach.

Mr. Amberley walked to Clarissa's side and bent toward her ear. "If it takes my last breath, I will see you and Duncan..." he hesitated, "part."

She gasped as Duncan approached her, and his brother ambled away, carrying a cup of punch.

"Sweetheart," Duncan said.

~ * ~

Once at her new home, Clarissa glanced out the bay window of the large stone house, which overlooked a stretch of woods.

Her lip trembled in wondrous disbelief, and she recalled the day she first saw this grand building and felt like an outsider, less important than the finely dressed guests. Now she was here as mistress of this home. Her courtship and marriage had been a whirlwind.

She faced her husband.

You're my husband. From the moment I first saw you, my life changed.

The servants had lined up. Clarissa inhaled deeply. She wished to greet them and chat but only nodded as Duncan introduced her to the butler and the housekeeper who bowed and curtsied.

Their guests gone, Duncan led Clarissa up a large winding staircase. They went down a hallway. He paused at a door. She shivered with awareness of the approaching occurrence. She loved him, so why was she so nervous? This was going to be a wonderful experience, was it not? Harriet assured her it would be if the man loved her.

Duncan pushed open the door. Once inside, he shut it behind them. Silver moonlight filtered in between billowing pink curtains. Duncan and Clarissa walked past a large wardrobe.

He guided her to the foot of the four-poster bed. "This is your room, and your dressing room is there." He tossed a glance behind her. "Your maid will help you with your toilette. I will come to you."

He skimmed his fingertips down her arm, leaning to kiss her. His fingers reached for her bodice. "Sweetheart, it's our wedding night. I must apologize for my enthusiasm."

"I love you, Duncan."

He kissed her softly, turned on his heel, and strode out of the room. She went to her nightstand and picked up a silver brush. A knock sounded at her door.

"Come in."

Her maid entered the room and helped her undress prior to brushing Clarissa's hair, curtsying, and then leaving her alone. Once Clarissa's shining hair hung down over the shoulders of her nightgown, she sat on the bed, awaiting her husband. He tapped on the door and entered, shutting it behind him.

"My love."

"My darling Clarissa." He came to her, and she stood.

Kissing her, he swept her up in his arms, lowered her onto the bed, and made tender love to her.

~ * ~

In the stables the next morning, Clarissa admired a gorgeous black mare, a gift from Duncan. "You are the best gift I have ever received."

"How endearing."

She turned and saw her brother-in-law with his mischievous expression.

"Clarissa, I must say, you are fetching."

"Mr. Amberley." She cast her glance downward.

He strode forward, uncomfortably close. She stepped back.

"I am informed on something you should be," Mr. Amberley said, with seduction in his voice.

She snapped her head up.

He inhaled sharply. "Do you draw the same reaction from your husband when you look up at him with those eyes?"

She frowned. "What do you want?"

"Are you curious to hear what I know, Clarissa?"

"No."

He fingered her cheek, and she backed against the mare.

"I shall tell you anyway, to prepare you because I care. My words at the wedding were nothing personal. I fear you married a man you don't really understand. He is still deeply frustrated. He walks around so tightly wound up he might explode. He aches to fondle you in his normal way, not a soft, tender way."

She trembled. *You're lying, but why? You scare me.*

"I don't blame you. I'd be terrified too. He's going to burst at any given time in the bedroom, mayhap even beat you for pleasure. I fear you are going to pay the price for his frustration. You see, I've seduced one or two of his former belles, and they have told me these things about him."

She could not command a word. *But what if Duncan is accustomed to more experienced women? I wish to enchant him more than any of his mistresses did.*

"If you have discomfiture and are afraid to let him near you, then come to me. I will be gentle with you."

Her fists became tight balls. "Get out of here! I love Duncan and will on no occasion go to another man!"

"We'll see." He smirked. "I'm worried for you. He's bragged to me of his history. Let me teach you how to manage him."

"Go away and worry yourself no further on my behalf."

"Sacrifice yourself to his wild passions if you love him so much. What's a bit of pain?" He growled suggestively. "Obviously, you do not care about your own well-being. My poor sweet, naïve sister, too eager to satisfy your husband."

"Leave me!"

With a smug smile on his handsome face, he turned around. "He has a secret, *sister*. Try to pry it from him." He walked away.

You strongly resemble your brother. Same green eyes—no, his are wiser, kinder. But the same dark-brown hair. No, he's more attractive. He's more muscular. You're soft, unused to work, and treacherous, a mad man, I'd venture. Duncan's a good man.

Anxiety rose up her throat. Mr. Amberley was a dangerous man.

Moments later Duncan came into the stables, smiling curiously. "Dear, I saw Ewan leaving. What did he want?" He touched her arm. She winced.

"Clarissa? What happened?"

"Your brother..."

"What about him?"

"He told me you, well, you…" She trembled.

He pulled away. "Clarissa?" His voice was tight with concern.

"You would never hurt me, I mean, in your great desire." It was more of a question than a statement.

He cupped her cheek. "No," he said so softly she had to strain to hear. He gave her a sad but tender smile. "I would not harm you." The warmth in his tone sounded like a promise. Then his expression grew hard. "I will have a word with Ewan."

"Have you got anything you wish to tell me?"

"Clarissa? I do not comprehend what you mean."

She gazed down. "I mean, now that we're married, you could tell me." She glanced up.

"No. Nothing." Sincerity rang true in his voice.

"Would you mind if I visited Harriet?"

"Of course not, sweetheart. Allow me to escort you."

~ * ~

Later that day their carriage drew to a halt outside the shop. Duncan helped Clarissa down onto the pavement.

"I'll be at the coffeehouse." He pointed down the road and drove away.

Clarissa walked into the shop, went through the curtain at the rear, and climbed the stairs. At the top, she entered her brother's apartment where Harriet sat on a small couch, sipping tea. Clarissa's heart jumped with gladness. Harriet, in yellows and blues, reminded Clarissa of a summer day on which the sun shone from a blue sky. Harriet's curls were piled high, but a loose ringlet hung by her ear.

Clarissa took off her bonnet. "I trust I find you well."

Harriet set the cup down and stood with her arms open. Clarissa slid into them, hugging her. They took a seat. Harriet regarded her with love.

"I have a question regarding something rather delicate. It concerns…lovemaking."

Harriet poured her tea. "Would you like a lemon-cheese tart?"

"No, thank you. To be honest, I have read forbidden books, and I cannot help wondering…" Her cheeks flushed.

"Go on. It's not as if we're quality. We can speak more openly."

She accepted the teacup from Harriet and took a sip. "We are educated and gentle, despite our origins."

"True, miraculously. However, you have my word I will not think less of you for speaking freely. Do not be afraid to talk to me."

Harriet's boldness jarred Clarissa, but she dismissed her uneasiness. She straightened, preparing to be bold herself. "I wonder if...I can increase Duncan's pleasure. Do you suppose he finds me boring? His former mistress, I mean, well, I wish to make him forget her. I'd like to try things without appearing shameless." She fidgeted.

Harriet patted her shoulder to encourage her.

"I shouldn't be discussing this. Proper ladies..."

Harriet scoffed. "You're not exactly a duchess. There's an East End accent simmering underneath your self-trained tones."

"I spent long hours listening to our cousin's tutor and imitating his speech. I may be a shopkeeper, but I am proper. I speak French, for goodness sake."

"And taught it to me. I had reservations concerning your husband leading up to the marriage, but is he good to you?"

"He's wonderful." She put her teacup on its saucer.

"I'm happy to hear that. Relieved. There must be an innocent explanation for my initial feelings about him. I'll give him the benefit of a doubt."

"He's a good man."

"How do I commence?" Harriet started. "A man can be *enthusiastic* without hurting you."

Clarissa gave her a weak smile. *If I can make him forget his former mistress, ask.* "When I go to him, how can I please him? What should I do first? I'm not sure about what I read in...certain books. You may not be familiar with the information either, but you've been married for years and have read things as well." With renewed embarrassment, she glanced down.

Harriet spoke, uttering wicked secrets of seduction, and Clarissa listened. Harriet informed her of things Duncan would appreciate but was too much of a gentleman to ask of her. The decadent topic grew

more so and drew her mind to a depraved man, and she thought of
Mr. Amberley and his threats to end her marriage.

"What is it?" Harriet uttered.

"His brother will do anything to ruin my marriage."

"He sounds dreadful."

"He's no gentleman. There's something odd about him. He's *more*
than troubled," Clarissa said.

"But has no power to end your marriage."

"Only the power to scare me."

Harriet's eyes narrowed. "I promise I will let no one hurt you."

Clarissa shuddered. Harriet's tone implied threat. How odd. She
could go from frightened to intimidating.

"What do you mean?" Clarissa asked.

"I have resources I'm not prepared to discuss."

"But—"

"Forget it, Clarissa."

Five

Light fell through a crack in the curtains alerting Clarissa to the new morning. She smiled, thinking of the advice Harriet had given her. At first, she'd had qualms about following her advice to arouse Duncan. She had gone slowly, one little caress at a time, letting her fingers and her tongue go a little further than last time. His surprised delight had encouraged more steps. She'd wait, then in the future stretch her exploration.

They faced each other, lying on their sides.

He intertwined his fingers with hers. "You are wicked, my wife, under the guise of being an angel." He guided her atop himself, and she yelped, chuckling. They made love again.

They dressed and had a wordless breakfast at their polished table. He watched her sensuously over his coffee, a gazette folded to his left. She nibbled her eggs.

"I have a meeting, sweetheart," he said.

"I'll see you tonight."

"Going to the shop?"

"I won't be long. Gilbert might require help."

"I would imagine he's enjoying prosperity, even without your excellent help on a daily basis."

"I do adore the shop, although I only work there a few days a month now."

"Then of course, I invite you to attend to your family business more often."

"On certain days, I may."

They stood, and he kissed her.

"Mmm," she moaned.

~ * ~

Duncan kissed his wife again and walked out the door, down the wide stairs, and to his office on the right side of the house, dreaming of his passionate wife, and unable to concentrate on the day ahead. She had released herself, as in his fantasies. After they spent their passion, they lay on the bed, astonished.

He had no idea marriage had the potential to be so ecstatic. He had assumed his desires could not be fully realized, secretly accepting that. But they were, and he was in awe.

Duncan paused at his office door and inhaled. *It has never been so amazing. Love makes the physical act intense.* He pushed open the door and went to his leather chair, sitting. He smelled the wax from the newly polished floor. His client entered, and Duncan presented him with a serious look.

"Mr. Tomy, have a seat." He gestured to the chair across from him.

"Captain, I have an offer I think you'll appreciate."

Clarissa's flushed face popped into Duncan's mind.

She rolled over and dragged her fingertips down my chest.

Duncan cleared his throat and attempted to push her out of his thoughts. His wife slipped into his imagination again, and he shifted in his chair, yearning for her. To dart out of his office, find her, and carry her to their bedroom...He gripped his armrests.

The meeting with the client was pointless. He hadn't retained a word.

"I'll be in touch." Mr. Tomy tipped his hat and left the office.

Duncan went to the stables.

Ewan discovered him there. "Brother, how is married life?"

He grinned.

"Her bed is that good, huh?"

He scowled and didn't answer.

"I'm surprised you're so happy. You're stuck with her."

"Thank God," he said, genuinely grateful. "She's mine for life..." he trailed off.

Ewan's eyes were so wide Duncan chuckled and patted his shoulder.

"Why the devil are you looking at me that way, Ewan?"

"Why are you so happy?"

"I love my wife."

"Oh?"

"Yes." *Madly*. Duncan let out a deep breath.

"Wives are rather dull, from what I've heard."

"Not mine. Do you remember me telling you about that mistress I once had from Paris?"

"Yes," Ewan said.

"I was walking around the deck of my ship for a month remembering that lady. I had recently attained a promotion. More of my thoughts were on that French girl than on my promotion."

"Have you been longing for her?"

"No. She does not compare to my wife."

Ewan gave him another wide-eyed look.

I don't think you'll ever realize what it's like to love a woman so entirely, so deeply you would not even consider touching another woman. Pity for Ewan coursed through him. "Sometimes I dream of running away with Clarissa."

Ewan burst out laughing.

He frowned. "What is so bloody funny?"

"You run the family business as tight as you ran your ship. You're widely recognized for your excellent occupational practices, so serious with the business. I'm shocked you would consider running away from it all. I'd be left behind to actually do the bloody work again. I couldn't be a man of leisure."

His brother's jests inspired Duncan to sigh in exasperation. He rubbed his face. Ewan and his ever-changing moods never ceased to amaze him. "You're a younger son. Choose a respectable profession, for God's sake, or, if only you'd help me run the business now that I'm home."

"I didn't come here to argue."

"You can't be a wastrel your whole life."

Anger flared in Ewan's expression. "Stop!"

Duncan wasn't up for a fight. He would address this issue for the thousandth time later.

"Let's go riding, Ewan."

"Yes."

While preparing their horses, Duncan reflected on the recent tension between him and his brother. He aspired to get things out in the open but started out lightly to put Ewan at ease.

"I can't stop thinking about Clarissa."

Ewan stared at him.

"Say something."

"I can't. I'm shocked."

"You're shocked?"

"Yes. I wonder if she has special motives."

He frowned. "Do not doubt her."

"Hmm."

"You are aware of how much our mother loved our father and he her."

"Yes. I remember them in their factory ownership days, how he regarded her, and how she looked at him with love. She'd tell him to raise the wages of the workers, and he did her bidding. I even remember how she'd bring those happy workers extra food and clothes, and Father rewarded her with looks of respect and adoration. It's a wonder he didn't lose his money with those practices Mother urged him to do."

Duncan swung onto his horse as Ewan did the same. They commenced out and took it at a slow pace.

"We'll circle the estate."

"It's cold, Duncan."

"Is your coat not adequate?" he teased.

"It is."

"Ewan, do you ever hope for true love with a woman?"

"Well that's a bit deep, don't you think?"

"Dare to experience it, that's what I have to say to you."

"I only need what's between the sheets."

"The best of that only comes when a woman loves you with the deepest of love."

They made their way across snow-covered countryside.

"You're in a fine mood today, talking to me like this," Ewan said. "I can't love in that way. We were born different, and everyone loved you. I was cast off."

"Not by our parents and not by me or our brothers."

Ewan reined in his horse, and so did Duncan.

"I miss them."

"So do I, Ewan. If it were in my power, I'd bring them back. I cannot stop regretting what happened."

"Ned's death is your fault."

He gripped his reins. "It is not!"

"Yes, Duncan, it is! You sent that letter even understanding he had a weak heart."

Duncan tightened his jaw. "You do wish to hurt me then."

"James died in battle, and Ned was in the way of you inheriting everything."

Duncan tugged his reins, and the brothers moved forward, passing a cottage.

"You stand in the way—" Ewan stopped himself from finishing his sentence.

"Pardon me?"

"Of my happiness."

Duncan shuddered. He doubted that's what Ewan had been thinking.

"You constantly harass me to go into a profession, which would hinder my contentment. You're a terrible brother."

"Are siblings supposed to do such harm to each other? Why do you do this to me?"

Ewan shrugged. "I'm sorry."

"You're forgiven. We should be friends."

Ewan trotted ahead, crunching over snow.

Duncan caught up to him. "Talk."

A pretty woman scampered across the snow carrying a basket. Ewan leered at her. She disappeared into her small cottage.

"She's delicious."

"What?" Duncan snapped.

"Try her, Duncan. You won't regret it."

"I will not go to her. I am married."

"So?" It came out on a chuckle.

"Our father and mother were faithful to each other. I overhead a conversation as a boy to confirm this."

"Perhaps it was an act, Duncan, something that parents do in front of their children."

He shook his head in disbelief. "Why do you say such a thing?"

"Do you remember our former, *beautiful* Auntie Hilda?"

Caution alerted him. "Yes. She was married to our Scottish uncle."

"She tucked me into bed often with sweet words. That was, brother, around the time I first noticed girls."

He studied him.

"Are you aware of why our uncle and aunt separated?" Ewan asked.

"No."

"Let me tell you. She seemed dedicated to our uncle, did she not?"

"Yes."

Ewan scoffed. "I caught her."

"You caught her doing what?"

"I was out playing, running around the moors, dreading the haggis that our grandfather dwas going to make me taste for supper that evening. I wandered toward our uncle's home. He was hunting. Then I saw Auntie Hilda and went to see her, but I stopped suddenly and hid behind the neighboring barn.

"A man approached her. She kissed him. They went into the barn. Moments later, she came out, her clothes untidy. The man came out after her and left quickly."

The great house came into view, and they turned toward it.

"You didn't say much for the rest of our visit. I can understand why, but Ewan, you were an angry boy. You had a short temper and created conflict. You ran away twice, even prior to Aunt Hilda marrying into the family."

"You should have made an effort to respect my feelings at the time. Father thought so highly of you, and as for me, well…"

"What is it concerning our *aunt* that bothered you?"

"She was young, Duncan, and I dreamt of kissing her."

Duncan gestured in dismissal. "Everyone knew that!"

Ewan wrapped resentful fingers around the reins. "What? Her duplicity shattered my trust in women, damn you. I informed our uncle of her treachery later. He sent her packing without so much as a goodbye." He huffed. "Now take me seriously for once. I demand it!"

"You often acted like a spoiled brat. You didn't have to make things so hard on our family."

"You'll pay for your disrespect, for your damn arrogance toward me, your own brother." Ewan hit his chest with his fist. "You didn't have to steal the glory, be the hero of our whole damn town."

"Is this what it's always been about?"

"No."

"Good, because you could have joined me aboard that ship, if not in another respectable profession, and earned glory."

"No thank you. I'm not stupid."

"And I am?"

Ewan scorned him. "You risked your life constantly. Why did I need to?"

"For love of country."

"We might have been French, for all I care."

Up shot Duncan's brows. "We are quite different."

"I agree."

"Still, I hope you find love eventually. It is the most rewarding experience a man can have."

"There is a woman who often slips into my mind. I had a memorable experience with her. She had blonde hair and blue eyes."

Duncan glanced at his brother. "Why not call on her now?"

Ewan's lips curved up impishly. "Now brother, you'd not approve. You see, she's married."

He huffed, and his breath emerged in a puffy cloud in the chilly air.

"To me, controlling a woman completely would be rewarding," Ewan went on.

Duncan sat straighter on the saddle. What an odd brother he had.

"I derive pleasure from pleasing myself and seeing a woman's concession to my whims in her cowering. Now you look angry, and you have no right to, Duncan. I see complete obedience for you in Clarissa's face, and I'm convinced you love it. You told me yourself that Clarissa would sacrifice her life for you."

You're a wickedly bold brother. "You don't have the slightest understanding. I don't control her, nor do I wish to. I am pleased because she is happy."

"You do control her, or she controls you. If I ever start to love a woman, I will fight it. I won't be restricted but must be in charge. When a woman begins to assume too much with me, I let her go."

Duncan scoffed. "We will not agree, but we don't have to. Brothers can disagree without hating each other."

"Like the English and the Americans?"

"Yes. You care for us, our family."

"Yes."

"Why have you caused so much trouble?"

Ewan's scrutiny followed another maid scampering into her cottage. He glanced back at Duncan. "Come now, is it not enough the town sees you as the hero? Do you still insist on being the savior of our family as well, rendering me the perpetual villain?"

"You're not the villain, merely the one who caused trouble, unendingly. Mother and I care for you, if you must make me say it, as did Father and our brothers." He shifted in the saddle, uncomfortable with this line of talk but supposed it was necessary with his unusual brother.

"Most of the time we got on well," Ewan said.

"Yes we did, but several times your antics hurt Mother."

"Father was strictest with me."

"No. He expected more of me than you and told me so."

"He on no occasion whipped you. He whipped me on several occasions."

"I did not give him cause to whip me, Ewan."

"It wasn't fair."

"I did not sell his prize horse for gambling money or bring a whore under his roof. I did not destroy a guesthouse with a wild, weeklong orgy, Ewan. That was embarrassing to the family."

"I was young."

"So was I."

Ewan sneered. "You sought amusement too and were not once whipped."

"Name one thing I did that warranted a whipping, because I promise you, if I had, I would have received a worse one than you ever did."

"Nothing comes to mind, but I'm sure there was something."

"The whippings should have toughened you up."

Ewan urged his horse to a stop under a towering tree, and Duncan challenged him with a commanding look.

"You insult me again. I suppose you're an example of manhood because you fought on the high seas. Whereas I only pranced around the estate engaged in pleasurable activities."

"Ewan."

His brother pulled his reins. "You're stronger, can run faster—"

Duncan lifted his palm to him. *What are you, a woman? I have to reassure you?* "Enough. There are women who prefer a man with your appearance. You dress finer than I on most occasions."

"You have a point. I seem more an educated gentleman than you do. You appear to be the enlisted younger brother."

"And I was not totally innocent, but I was never a little heathen."

"You can go to the devil."

"I did not mean to insult you again. Accept my apology."

Ewan glared at him.

"Do you remember any of our good times?"

Grudgingly, Ewan nodded. "There were a few."

"More than a few." He forwarded his horse, and Ewan rode beside him again.

"Do you recall our boyhood, the summer spent with our Scottish grandparents and—"

Ewan smiled. "And I lost my way, wandering around the highlands by myself, following lost sheep."

"I went searching for you, calling out your name."

"I heard you, Duncan. It was dark, and I called to you. You didn't hear me tell you to be careful."

"I fell over that cliff and lay on the ground hurt. You helped me."

"I was scared. You were bleeding. I thought you might die, and that disturbed me."

"Even so, you told me I was going to recover. You helped me to stand. I propped against your shoulders as we walked, maybe for an hour. We talked and joked. Someone finally came across us. You were brave that day." Duncan tossed him a glance, understanding he indulged his brother because he had lost the others, and deep down, he did blame himself for Ned's sudden death.

They stayed silent for the rest of the way back.

~ * ~

Troubled, Ewan's smile turned into a frown as ambivalent emotions overcame him. He loved his brother, but he resented him. A powerful urge shot through him. Tense, he glanced at Duncan. Was he capable of doing something that was swelling into a fierce hunger? His pulse raced. He thought of the unbelievably pretty Clarissa.

There's no justice in the world. You won her. It should have been me. I will hurt you, Duncan, and I will do it through your wife.

Six

Clarissa swallowed her laughter and put a finger to her lips. Duncan strode across his private stable, having dismissed the servants, and kissed Clarissa. They fell into a large hay pile, still kissing. She tickled him. He laughed and tickled her back, drawing giggles. Moments later, he slid up her gown, unbuttoned his trousers, and they were making love.

"Who are you?" she asked afterwards, teasing him.

He grinned in a reproachful way, holding her and dragging lazy fingers up and down her arm. "Are you such a light skirt you have forgotten already?"

"I...can't seem to remember. I pray you're my husband."

He kissed her. "I relish sweeping you away. Your name is Clarissa Amberley, thank God."

"I love you."

"I love you too."

"The big oak is next," she said under lowered lids.

"Something to look forward to, my love! You're exhilarating."

~ * ~

Clarissa rolled over in bed. "Good morning, beloved."

"Good morning. Breakfast. I won't be five minutes after you."

"May you be indescribably happy," she whispered to him moments later as she walked into the small attached dressing room where her maid waited to assist with the morning toilette.

"Betty, really, I can do this myself. I have been for years."

The young maid curtsied, her blonde curls bouncing under the edges of her cap. "Madam, it is my honor to serve you."

"Very well. Thank you."

When Clarissa went to the main dining room and took a seat, she started, seeing her brother-in-law and his lascivious smirk. He stepped closer, standing in her personal space. Heaviness fell upon Clarissa's shoulders, and she pressed her lips into a line.

"My, my, Clarissa. You appear as though you have experienced a night of intense passion. Your cheeks glow a becoming pink."

You're mad. She burned with embarrassment and fear.

"Duncan has never smiled so much. It's unbelievable. It's scandalous, considering his guilt over..."

"Over what?"

"Tell me what you—"

She gulped. "It is none of your concern."

"I'm his brother."

She glared at him as anger squashed her previous alarm. "You are no gentleman, Mr. Amberley!"

He slanted closer. "Is there any chance you might have some of that passion left for me? Stun me, Clarissa."

She bounded to her feet, her chair screeching across the floor. She glanced around; tempted to find the heaviest thing she could lift and whack him.

Duncan entered the room, smiling. "Darling." He took his seat.

Her anger and indignation melted in an instant. "Duncan," she uttered, angling her head in his brother's direction.

"Oh, my apologies, Ewan. I did not see you here. In Clarissa's presence, I'm mindful of nothing else." He glanced around. "Where are the footmen?"

"I dismissed them on an errand."

On the chance you'd find me alone?

"Why?" Duncan asked.

"I pity you."

How would Duncan respond?

With a twitch of his lips, he spoke to his brother. "How odd. I pity *you!*"

Mr. Amberley sneered and strode out of the room.

~ * ~

Ewan shut the door to Duncan's office and poured them both drinks. He presented him with a glass of whiskey and toasted him, taking a seat across from him.

"Brother."

Duncan smiled.

"My God, man, you look like a schoolboy. She's merely a woman."

Duncan choked on his whiskey. "You jest. She's not simply a woman. You have seen her."

"According to you, beauty isn't the most important thing."

"True, true, but I've had some really agreeable mistresses in the past. Clarissa is so much more to me, a companion. We have intriguing conversations in front of the hearth at night."

"You cannot be serious."

"I am." *You would be surprised. She has friends she exchanges letters with across the globe. She writes to people in America and at least a dozen other countries as well and has read rare books. Hearing her secrets, I swear to keep silent.*

Ewan gave him a mocking look.

"She has a sense of humor. My lovely wife makes me happy."

"Yes, because she satisfies you so deeply in bed at night."

Anger shot through him. His brother went too far. He tapped a fist on his polished desk. "That's enough."

"People are talking."

"What do you mean?"

"At the club, Duncan. My Navy friend told me so. Why does a wealthy gentleman allow his wife to work? Why do you allow her so much freedom? You treat your woman better than you treat your best thoroughbred, and it is widely recognized you treat your horses well."

He gestured toward a painting of a splendid stallion on the wall to the left.

Duncan chuckled lightly then swallowed more whiskey.

"What is so amusing?" Ewan crossed an ankle over his knee.

"Tell me, if you had a woman like Clarissa, would you take the light from her countenance?"

"I…"

"Well? She'd die inside, and our love as well."

"I wouldn't care. I would control her. She would have to live with whatever decision I made for her."

He toasted his brother. "Here's to you then, Ewan, as my brother, despite your different ways, which I often despise. Find yourself a woman like Clarissa, take away her passion, and discover that nothing will be left over for you. I'm not a fool. I'm not one of the Prince Regent's advisors for nothing."

Ewan filled his glass to the rim and gulped it down. "Sometimes I worry about you. First you give away your chance at further promotion by letting those Americans go. After your hard work, your exceptional valor saw you made post captain younger than anyone else in history… you turned the king's eye toward you and could expect more." Ewan steepled his fingers in his lap. "You let your wife do whatever she will. Unbelievable, as bossy as you are. You seem to be protective of the family, and me, but in doing so, you're often controlling. Who is the smarter of the two of us, Duncan?"

Duncan passed his hand through the air. "See it as you will. Do you not think Clarissa would not do my least bidding?"

Ewan raised his brow. "Careful, brother, or your wife might chance by and hear you say such words," he mocked.

"I do not mean that in the manner in which you are taking it. She is so agreeable, so sweet and charming…" He cleared his throat. "She is happy to accommodate me. We don't argue. I give her the smallest request, and she rushes to do as I ask."

"You do the same for her." Ewan sipped his drink.

"I do, and I'm happy to do so."

"You sicken me. A man should save that for his mistress and have dignity in his relationship with his wife."

"Fine words coming from you. You won't let yourself experience the great joy of monogamous love. You have spent your time gambling and womanizing."

"What the deuce have you seen around the globe to make you so strange?"

Me strange? You're a devilish odd character. "Happily married men and their adoring wives."

"Whilst you were out saving the world, you had your share of women. Spare me, brother."

Duncan sat forward in his leather chair. "You still do those things. You have been through twice the women as I have, and you're younger! And I've traveled the world! Don't you grow weary or bored?"

"I don't need to work like Father. You are stuck with that and choose to be tied to one woman."

"The one I want. I'm overseeing the family business, and it is a rewarding occupation. You think you are smarter, and I think that I am more fortunate." His smile widened.

Ewan put his glass down. "Good day."

Seven

A few weeks later, during the slow hours, Duncan took Clarissa to the shop and went for coffee. He joined her presently, striding into her family's establishment. To his surprise, Mrs. Hale was beside her, chatting. Delighted to see his sister-in-law finally venturing out, he noticed Gilbert was nowhere to be seen—probably on a professional errand. No one currently patronized the shop either, as three customers had moments ago walked out the door with packages.

Duncan went to Clarissa, kissed her hand, and turned to Mrs. Hale, tipping his hat. "Good day."

"Good day," Mrs. Hale said, with a wavering smile.

"How do you do?" he asked.

She didn't answer. A bit of discomfort traveled through him. Clarissa had told him in private that Mrs. Hale had disappeared for months, and on her return, acted the part of a changed woman. Something frightening had happened to her.

He sought to put her at ease. "Among my friends, I esteem your husband the most."

Mrs. Hale gave him a raised-brow look. "Truly?"

He relaxed, happy she seemed to. "Yes. I must say I have a great deal of regard for him. He's a funny fellow, too. I find myself laughing in his company, or whenever I visit Clarissa at her family business, and Gilbert and I converse. He told me amusing stories recently. I am happy to have joined our families." He tapped the countertop with his fingers.

"As am I," Clarissa said.

"Gilbert is as much my brother as Ewan ever was. And you are now my sister. Clarissa and I shall host a special dinner party for you and your husband. Would you like that?"

Mrs. Hale and Clarissa smiled.

"We'll make a grand evening of it to celebrate the happy joining of our families."

"Yes, I would like that very much. Thank you. Has Mr. Hale told you about the funny thing that happened on our wedding day?"

"No. What happened?"

"Well," Mrs. Hale began, "we had finished with the special outdoor ceremony. Clarissa looked up. She saw my cousin Brian directly for the first time that day. He was so startled by the unusual color of her eyes that he fell back into a brand new, giant pile of..."

Suddenly the door opened, the bells tinkling, and in walked Ewan. "Duncan, a footman told me I could find you here. I need a favor."

Mrs. Hale backed away, white with shock, and she huddled behind her sister. Ewan snarled. Mrs. Hale moaned and buried her face against Clarissa's shoulder.

Clarissa whirled around and hugged her. "Harriet, what's wrong?"

"It's him!"

"What are you talking about?" Clarissa asked.

"He abducted me!"

"Don't be ridiculous," Ewan replied and glanced at Duncan. "She's a lunatic."

"Clarissa, don't let him near me!"

Duncan offered a soothing gesture. "Mrs. Hale, calm down. You're mistaken. This is my brother."

"Was he at home every month of last year?"

"No. He was overseas for some time, but..."

"It's him, I tell you!"

Ewan scowled. "You are a stupid girl and have mistaken me for another."

Mrs. Hale faced Clarissa. "Sister, it is he!"

Clarissa's fists rested at her sides. Confusion and fear washed over her features. She then straightened and glared at Ewan, retreated from Mrs. Hale's grip, and approached him. She slapped him.

He raised his hand to hit her.

Duncan gripped his wrist then released it. "You will never lay a hand on my wife," he threatened. He turned to Clarissa. "It couldn't have been him."

"Why, because he is your brother?"

"Yes!"

"Duncan, if Harriet says it was him, then it was."

"She's mistaken, my dear."

"I am not!" Mrs. Hale dared, from behind Clarissa.

He brought his gaze to her, annoyed, but sympathetic. "Mrs. Hale, a mistake has been made."

"Yes, it has," Ewan said. "I swear it on my family honor."

Duncan considered him. Ewan's expression spoke of truth and desperation. Frequently a boorish man, and cork-brained more often than not, he still couldn't be the evil person Mrs. Hale accused him of being. Duncan wouldn't believe his troubled brother was *that* troubled.

"No, I'm certain," Mrs. Hale said.

"I'm sending word to the magistrate," Clarissa said.

Images of Ewan rotting in prison and succumbing to jail fever or worse, being hanged, shot through his mind. Pictures of his mother crying in his arms, losing the third of four sons, sent a shudder to Duncan's soul. "You will do no such thing."

Clarissa's brow came up. "You would stop me?"

"With force if necessary. I'll lock you up if I have to. You are my wife, and I can do whatever I will with you," he said, and immediately regretted those words. He sounded like his brother to his own ears, but he was terrified for Ewan, and even more so for their mother.

This didn't have to happen, not over a misunderstanding, an accusation from a good woman who was obviously ill. He could offer to hire someone to find the real villain and opened his mouth to say so.

Clarissa slapped Duncan. With great surprise, he touched his stinging cheek then reached for her arm in question.

His wife took a giant step backwards. "I won't report him yet, but I will gather my own evidence to make certain the law punishes him. Get out of my shop, Captain, and take your reprobate brother with you!"

She turned to her sister-in-law. "Harriet, do we have a slate back there? I could hang it from my neck with the word 'Dunce' chalked on it. I should have put the pieces together." She cried, facing Duncan. "Your brother resembles you, and Harriet had a bad reaction to you that first night."

"Believe your husband above all else," Duncan uttered.

"How can I?"

"Trust my judgment on this. I'm not related to a madman. He's bold and strange, but not a lunatic or a criminal. Mrs. Hale is mistaken, obviously ill."

"I want to trust your judgment on this, but I don't." She sniffled.

"You betray me."

Ewan dragged him, stumbling backward, toward the door.

"Clarissa," Duncan muttered.

"Trust *my* judgment, Duncan." She reached toward him.

"I can't. You're blind."

She burned him with her glare.

"Witch," he accused, glaring back at his wife.

Eight

Walking past the shop, Duncan saw Clarissa for the first time in weeks. She had returned to her family. He peeked in the window and saw her smiling in discussion with a customer. He recalled his first time seeing her, when she had looked up at him.

"My God, do I love her."

Visions of the last look she gave him and her lack of faith in his judgment had him cringing. He dashed away. "I will not surrender to a woman." *I've faced Bonaparte's men and will not be conquered by a pair of seductive blue-green eyes!*

He hurried home and dined with Ewan. Their mother turned in early, feeling not quite the thing.

Duncan didn't touch his beef while unconsciously tapping his fingers on the table. "Ewan."

"What is it?" He held his fork.

"I can't forget her." *She fascinates me. She's interesting, beautiful, and passionate enough even for me, rare.* "I'm trying to banish her from my mind, but I cannot." *I yearn for her constantly.*

Ewan poured wine into his glass and pushed the bottle across the table. "You're her husband. Drag her home."

"I will not do that. I respect her."

"So? Demand that she come home. Grab her, throw her into your carriage, kicking and screaming if you have to, and toss her into your room. Lock it up, and let her pound on the door until her hands bleed."

"You don't grasp what love is."

Ewan glared. "Maybe I do!" His words came out with resentment more than truth, Duncan realized.

"Do you, now?"

"It's conceivable. Your marriage was consummated. She has no recourse."

He sat back, seeing that Ewan hoped to bring the topic around to his favorite subject.

"I'll wager bedding her is unbelievably satisfying." Ewan smirked.

Duncan stretched his arms out and rested them on the chair's sides.

"Is she exceptionally soft, more so than other women?"

Duncan did not answer.

"She is a shopkeeper, not a fine lady. Does she do unusual things to you?"

Mild alarm and anger made him grasp the armrests of his chair. "Stop it. You speak of my wife and go too far."

"Well, I'm your brother."

"Why do you ask me something so deeply personal?"

"Clarissa is the loveliest woman I have ever encountered. You were dark and serious before meeting her." He twirled his fork gleefully. "Then one day I saw you smiling over your paperwork. The next day I saw lightness in your step. You told me you were going to visit a shop to check on one of your collections. You eagerly anticipated going there."

"Yes."

"Your disposition grew lighter and lighter until you were a changed man."

"Yes."

"Then, Duncan, you married, extremely tense, desperate to caress her, anyone could see."

Duncan inhaled slowly.

"After you had her, you walked around like you had died and gone to heaven. Good God, Duncan, I must hear what that goddess would do to you. I have not seen a man more moved than you."

He studied Ewan.

"Duncan?"

"Do you really wish for details?" He asked in warning, his eyes narrowing.

Ewan took the hint. "Either go and get her and keep her locked up, or forget her. But you should bring her back."

"Hoping to catch us in the act?"

"Of course not." He glanced away briefly. "Go fetch her, not for me, but because you are so in love with her."

He let out a deep sigh. "Keep pushing me. I may endeavor to coax her back tonight, but you should keep your filthy mind to yourself, brother." He rubbed his forehead in frustration. "Ewan, what was Gilbert's wife talking about?"

"I don't know."

"Or is it that you won't tell me?"

Ewan shrugged. "I mean it. I have no idea."

Duncan searched his brother's mien and got no hint of deception.

"I have a friend," Ewan said. "I could hire a person to look into things and find out what really happened."

"I suggest you do, as I will, separately. We need to have evidence to prove your innocence. I will not go to Clarissa after all, tempted as I am, whilst she is convinced my brother is a criminal, not merely a—"

"Rather unpleasant situation, I mean, your ambivalence."

"It would break us apart again. No, I want her proven wrong first, to repent."

"I don't blame you."

Duncan finished his supper in silence.

~ * ~

That night, Duncan rolled over in bed, running fingers over the cold spot across from him, thinking of Clarissa. He should be leaning down, loving her, kissing her until she sighed in pleasure. In his mind she moaned aloud, digging her fingernails into his back and saying his name hotly against his neck. She would rub her legs against his sides, muttering little sounds and saying, "I love you, I love you, I *love* you." Duncan collapsed back as tremendous waves of sadness washed over his spirit.

He tensed his jaw, suddenly vexed. Gilbert left the shop on business from time to time, and men came in to make purchases. Clarissa would look up from her bookkeeping, and they would gasp. He saw it once; he did it when he met her.

Duncan threw off his blankets and sat up. He could demand she give up her work. No, not an option, not considering the promise he made that he never would.

~ * ~

Clarissa slit the paper off a long package a courier had delivered to the shop.

"What's that?" Gilbert asked.

"It came originally from America. Took a long route here. There are books and other items inside, and a surprise for you."

"Oh?"

She lifted out a finely polished wooden walking stick with a silver-capped top. "I thought you'd like this."

"Thank you." His voice spoke of his admiration. He reached for the gift, running fingertips over the surface. "This was expensive."

"You are welcome."

He grinned.

"That's not all. I have a book for you in here somewhere." She rummaged through the contents. "Ah, here it is!" She gave him a brand new military book.

He accepted it gratefully. "Clarissa..."

"I knew you'd like it since you couldn't sign up for service due to your—"

"Lame leg. My friends serve."

She touched his shoulder. "You're not too disappointed anymore?"

"No, not so much. Besides, Harriet really needs me at home. Something upset her recently. She won't tell me what it is. Has this anything to do with why you left Duncan? The timing coincides. You still won't discuss the specifics?"

"No."

"He didn't beat you or keep a mistress?"

"No, I told you that."

"I was happy you married him. He seemed so right for you. Can you not excuse whatever he did?"

"Gilbert, it's more serious than you would imagine."

"Tell me more!"

"He defended his dreadful brother, sided against me, his wife, and threatened to lock me up!"

Gilbert tapped his walking stick on the floor once. "He didn't?"

"He did!"

"Did his brother hurt you?"

"No, but he did something horrible."

"Oh."

"Yes, oh. Do not ask more now. I'll enlighten you later."

"But—"

She fidgeted with a stack of papers on the counter. "I'm foolish for falling in love with Duncan."

"I don't believe that."

"I must go to the Exchange today."

"Why?"

"Acquisitions. I'm meeting an agent there. He has interesting artifacts for us and told me he'd be there anyway."

"Let me get my coat. Women are not usually seen there alone."

They stepped into the chilly air, quiet. Arriving at the Exchange later, they waited in the predetermined spot.

Gilbert excused himself. "I see an old chum from Islington. I'll stay close." He went off to join his boyhood friend.

~ * ~

Duncan arrived and dusted the snow off the sleeves of his elegant greatcoat. He glanced around the Exchange for his professional associate. His wife was there, fidgeting on her feet. A heavy load dropped onto his chest. He stared at her; she was beautiful in a plum-colored walking dress. So innocent with her unassuming countenance, wringing a dainty blue-green handkerchief, in the midst of this business pavilion. Her feminine appearance clashed with the wealthy, well-dressed gentlemen in their dark coats who presided over the grounds.

Turning, he saw his brother-in-law in modest, middling-class attire, leaning on an expensive walking stick, and talking to what appeared to be a friend.

Duncan knew Clarissa had saved her money for months. With a beaming smile, she had told him over supper about the beautiful present she had ordered for her brother.

"Duncan?" Gilbert drew his attention.

"Hello."

"This is a surprise. My sister…" He faltered and cleared his throat.

"Your sister what?"

"Clarissa misses you."

"Did she say this?"

"No. She said you did not defend her."

Duncan clenched his jaw. "I'm afraid I went against my heart."

"Go talk to her."

"I will. Good day."

"Good day."

Duncan walked away, his brow furrowed in confusion. "Clarissa did not tell him," he mumbled.

She looked up and saw him. He stopped, startled. The sad bluish-green luminescence of her eyes, underneath long lashes, gave him pause.

"My God. She did it to me again." With hesitant steps, he reached her and cleared his throat. He tipped his hat gingerly. "Madam, Clarissa, my wife."

Nine

There in the middle of the Exchange, Clarissa watched Duncan with a trembling lower lip. He gestured to a corner away from the crowds. She followed.

"Have you come to apologize?" She tugged at her velvet bonnet strings, retying them.

"What?" he snapped. "No!"

"Then what?"

"I miss you. Nothing's right without you. It's colder and lonelier in my home than my cabin after a night of fighting, and my friends injured or dead."

She stared at him.

He tensed his features. "But you, Clarissa, owe me an apology. Make it and come home." His heart softened. "Please come home."

"An apology?" She edged away from him. "How do you suppose I owe you that?"

He tore one of his gloves off, then the other, and gripped them. "You defied me, your husband. You sided against me." His lips formed a tight line in his sudden anger.

She exhaled through her nose. "Are you jesting? You refused to champion your wife!"

"Clarissa." He grasped her arm. "Know your place!"

The tears overflowed onto her cheeks. "I was under the impression you respected me." She looked around, side to side. "Where is that 'Dunce' slate of mine?"

"Dash it! You were not dim-witted for falling in love with me. In fact, you are a clever person, and that is among the reasons you have stolen my heart."

"You can't really feel that way."

"I do. If I only desired you for your beauty...I want you to be the mother of my children, to give me intelligent, strong, good children." He glowed with respect for her. "You stimulate my mind as well as my body. It thrills me to have a rare woman such as yourself."

"Well, darling," she mocked, "then I fear you have a worthy adversary!" She gripped her reticule.

"What do you mean?"

"I shall defeat your brother. I read in the *Gazette* a story on a certain earl who led a similar enquiry with success. I'll approach him with the evidence I gather. Bide your time."

He pointed to her. "I will not allow that to happen. I will protect him till the end, Clarissa!"

"But he is an abductor."

"He is not!" he enunciated. "Don't you realize what those accusations would do to my family?"

"I thought I was your family."

"You're impossible!"

"So are you!" She spun with a swish of her skirt.

"I will not allow Ewan to be renounced. I will not lose my last brother." Thoughts of his lost siblings weighed heavily on him. How could he ever let that happen again? He turned, stiff-backed, and walked out.

~ * ~

A week later, three customers left the Hale shop with their purchases, so Clarissa went over her accounting at the main counter. Bells tinkled at the door. In walked Duncan, a ray of sunlight playing off his dark brown hair as he pushed the door open. Cold air rushed in, and the sounds of horses' hooves clip-clopping behind him quieted when the door swung closed. His greatcoat hung open.

He looked wonderful in a new pair of trousers and dark coat, unadorned but of the most exquisite cut. A waistcoat embroidered with lavish designs covered linen of the snowiest white, and a well-starched neck cloth topped off his elegant ensemble.

He strode to her and bowed without warmth. Clarissa pretended to dust a pile of books resting to her right. Her insides whirled, and her cheeks flushed. Love burned brightly for her husband. She cursed silently, having betrayed herself.

"Mrs. Amberley, your and Mrs. Hale's presence are required, at your earliest convenience. New information has been discovered."

"On the morrow. Here."

"Ewan and I must discuss something with you."

She straightened her spine. "Come at closing time. Have him wait outside, and do not do this until you see Gilbert leave on an errand. He's uninformed of this situation."

He focused on her hand, gently brushing it with his fingers. Would he raise her fingers to his lips for a kiss? He did not.

Clarissa turned away to hide her treacherous tears. He left. Someone called out to her, Gilbert, from behind the shop. She had barely heard his muffled voice. *He must have many boxes and needs my help.*

She glanced at the front door. Not a patron within view. "I'll be quick." She went for the back door of the building to open it for her brother. Peering through the crack, she didn't see him at first and stepped outside. He was picking up boxes to her left. She bent to help him, and sudden tears spilled onto her cheeks.

Gilbert's brow crinkled.

"He was here." She uttered a little sob.

"Duncan."

"Yes."

~ * ~

After walking a few yards, Duncan stopped and turned back to the shop, prickles crawling up his spine inspired by vague sounds of crying. He made his way around and leaned against the brick wall to conceal himself. Clarissa was crying, and Gilbert was hugging her.

"I'm a stupid girl! I long for my husband. Seeing him today and at the Exchange a week ago, I wanted to throw myself into his arms. I have little control of my feelings when he is close. I'm such a goose!"

"You're not stupid or a fool. Duncan is a good man. Whatever he did, he has the integrity to have an excellent reason for it."

"His brother will pay a high price for what he did."

Duncan inhaled sharply.

"Certain parties involved have given me new information, Gilbert. It seems Mr. Amberley is guilty of more than I thought."

"If that's so, then rest assured Duncan is not involved."

"I don't even think he believes his brother is capable of doing anything wrong to that degree. He believes he's innocent, as rag-mannered as he is."

"Right, or why else would Duncan give you up to defend him? He fears for his brother in a big way, that's the only explanation."

"If it were something else…thievery, pirating, you name it, I would forget it because I love Duncan. But this is serious, Gilbert."

"Tell me when you're ready."

"I will."

He escorted her back into the building.

~ * ~

The next evening, Clarissa saw Harriet send Gilbert off to purchase more watercolors. In the dim shop, oil lanterns cast a weak glow over shelves of books and trinkets. Duncan approached the front door, shaking snow from his shoulders. Harriet squeezed Clarissa's arm.

Clarissa glanced at her. "Do not worry."

A smile of gratitude came to Harriet's lips. "I could at all times count on you. I need to now."

Duncan strode through the door and removed his hat, glancing at both of them. "Clarissa, may I have a private word with you first?" He looked over at Harriet and gave her a smile. "Mrs. Hale, I promise to return her shortly."

"It will be fine," Clarissa promised. She padded over the cool floor in her slippers and locked the door. With a nod, she stepped into a shadowed corner near the front. A lantern cast a low flickering light on Duncan's face.

"Duncan..."

"I like hearing you use my given name."

Kiss me. She bit her lip. "What is this concerning?"

"Please drop this. You wouldn't have my brother's life ruined, would you? You love me. This would kill my mother. I've lost too many in my family already. My father died for England, and my elder brothers—"

"I don't want to hurt you, but I have to pursue this. Your brother injured my sister and did worse. It is my duty to present the facts to the authorities. I'm unhappy you have a brother like him. I'll make it up to you your whole life." She raised her chin. "I'll be the best wife and give you beautiful children."

Duncan frowned. "Only if you forget this nonsense." He touched her chin with his fingertips. "I must hear you're remorseful for ever having pursued this."

"I had a wonderful vision of you and me enjoying Christmas by a roaring fire, surrounded by happy children with dark hair like yours, and blue-green eyes like mine." She gave him a rueful smile. "You bouncing our youngest on your knee with cheer. I, barely able to contain my love for you as I kiss you." She felt her cheeks grow hot as she caught a glimpse of desire from him. "Then we would express our feelings alone."

He sighed.

"But you continue to side with him over me. You choose your brother over me, and Gilbert said you had the integrity to stand up for justice, the right thing." She rested fists on her hips.

"If my brother weren't innocent, I wouldn't have let you walk away." Duncan squeezed her arms. "You're important to me."

"Not as important as he is."

"This whole matter will ruin my family, Clarissa, and kill my mother."

She jerked back, but he held on. "You can't really believe he's innocent!"

"Yes!" He let go of her arms.

"Well, I'm relieved your honor is preserved."

He furrowed his brow.

"Duncan, if you believe you're doing right—" Her hand came to his wrist.

"I wish it were otherwise."

"What are you saying?"

"Can I have Ewan in?" He glanced toward the window.

"Only up front."

Duncan went outside. He came back with his brother, standing inside by the door. Clarissa glanced at Harriet who was peeking from behind the curtain.

Clarissa glared at Mr. Amberley. "What have you to say?"

"Hear me out."

"Only for this reason, Mr. Amberley, I love Duncan."

"Be gentle, Ewan. Clarissa is my wife," Duncan urged.

Ten

Duncan took in Clarissa under the low lantern light of her shop.

"Our investigation has revealed interesting things." Ewan rubbed his brow.

"Oh? Enlighten us," she said.

"It turns out there was this asylum," he continued.

Clarissa raised a brow. "Really?" she drawled.

Ewan twitched his lips. "Its Chief Medical Officer, Dr. Dearborn, is brilliant."

She played with a blue-green bow on her glove.

"Apparently, Mrs. Hale was injured somehow, forgot who she was, and wandered aimlessly until she was detected and placed in an institution."

"Clever lies indeed," Clarissa mocked.

Ewan tugged at his cuffs. "Somehow she managed to escape."

Clarissa curled her lip, scorning him. "When she came home, Mr. Amberley, she knew who she was."

"That could happen. Some patients do recover their minds, and without explanation. It is also possible her injury confused her for a time."

Clarissa studied him. Protective love warmed Duncan. She patted fists at her sides. Ewan shifted in his coat.

"My sister says, Mr. Amberley, that she had to cut through the docks late one night to arrive home after a friend failed to keep an appointment. She saw you there. What she said next is really rather fascinating."

Ewan swung away to stare out of the dark window.

She continued, her fingers uncurling. "You were talking to a street girl. The conversation became heated. You pushed her. She slapped you. You struck her hard across the face. She fell back onto a cargo of bricks waiting to be loaded. She wasn't moving. You placed your head on her chest and looked up, terrified. You took the brick that took her life and put it on her chest. You removed her skirt and used it to tie the brick around her and dumped her body into the water."

Duncan and Ewan both gaped at her.

"Mrs. Hale became terrified and ran from her hiding place. You heard her and ran after her. You caught her. You thought she was beautiful. You rendered her senseless and then...kept her." Her voice broke. "She escaped, eventually." Tears had thickened her voice.

Ewan scowled. "That is the most absurd thing I've ever heard in my life!"

Duncan stepped close to Clarissa's side.

Ewan's features tensed. "Brother, believe me. It's not true!"

Duncan took out his handkerchief and dabbed Clarissa's wet cheeks. "Maybe she is mistaken?"

"She is not. I believe her. Now believe me because you respect my judgment," she said in soft tones.

I look at you and do, my love. Despite my convictions, you have conquered me with your truth. "I do."

Pain faded from her face, and a smile brightened her countenance. "You do?"

"Yes, but I also believe Mrs. Hale speaks what she believes to be the truth. She's ill, sweetheart."

Ewan withdrew a piece of paper from his coat pocket. He pushed it toward her. "Dr. Dearborn, the director of the asylum, will testify that Harriet Hale was there for months. Here is his written testimony."

Clarissa scanned it. "I will discover the reason he chose to lie for you even if I face financial ruin to get the evidence to convict you."

"Clarissa, please," Duncan said.

"You'll face more than that!" Ewan barked.

Duncan whipped his head towards Ewan. He stepped in front of Clarissa with his arm across her chest protectively. "Ewan?"

"I'm...sorry. I'm...vexed. I will cooperate in your own investigation."

"What was that?"

"A mistake, Duncan. I didn't mean to disrespect your wife."

"She and I may be temporarily living apart, but I will not allow any harm to come to her or her family."

"You still believe me, don't you?" Ewan asked him.

"Yes, yes, I do, especially with Dr. Dearborn's testimony. We'll clear this up." He looked at Clarissa, lowering his arm.

"We can't all be telling the truth, Duncan!"

Was he to lose a fourth member of his family so soon after the death of his brothers and father—his last brother or his wife? Gripping sadness overtook him, but he reined it in, anxiously needing a peaceful solution to this.

"Allow me to get Mrs. Hale the finest treatment. I know a doctor who has done wonders in these cases."

"Duncan!"

"Sweetheart, we have the written testimony of the chief of the asylum. Let's end this now. I miss you."

"Why do you stand by the side of someone who doesn't share your sense of honor and decency?"

Ewan glared at her. Troubled, Duncan could not speak to her of the hidden depths there, the pain caused by his brother.

"I love you so much, Duncan. This kills me to do this. I do not defy you intentionally."

"Stop this now, I beg you."

She tensed her jaw. "Goodbye. It was beautiful being your wife. I'm wretched now that it's over." She sobbed and ran to Mrs. Hale, who still peeked from behind the shop curtain. She pulled Clarissa behind it.

Duncan's breathing became quick and shallow. The creak of footsteps on the wooden stairs leading up to their rooms made its way to his ears. He turned and saw Ewan staring at the curtain.

"Ewan, what are you thinking?"

"How unhappy I am for them both, for you. I never meant to come between you and your wife." He darted another glance at the curtain. "Go up there and take her home whether she likes it or not."

Duncan gaped. "I am a gentleman, not a barbarian. In the Navy, I have seen enough violence to last a lifetime and do not believe in abduction. I abhor it."

"Taking your own wife is not any kind of abduction."

"If she doesn't want to come along, it is."

"It is not."

"She's a person, Ewan."

"She's your property! My wife would be chained to my bed by now."

Duncan scoffed. "Like a slave. Good God man, this is the nineteenth century."

"You're a fool. You let a woman have such influence over you."

The woman of my dreams. The woman I think about every minute of the day. Yes, she has influence over me. "You're the fool for avoiding that kind of love."

Ewan stalked around the room. "You aren't going to support her, are you? I need your backing, or I'm finished. It's easy for you. You are a great naval hero, a champion. I, in contrast, am nothing. And because I did not serve! Bah!"

"No, no. You are selfish, that is your trouble. However, you are my brother. As a boy, I promised our mother I would continually stand by you. She seemed to sense you would need it. I'm deuced disappointed it's not working out for Clarissa and me. She's willing to lose me over this issue." *That devastates me.*

"Husbands have rights."

"So, you condone physical violence? Maybe you did hit the street girl."

"No, of course not. Maybe once or twice I slapped a woman but not to the extent of which I have been accused."

"You prepared to slap Clarissa."

"It was nothing. I would have barely touched her, I promise you. I would not have hurt your wife."

"I hope not. Women are to be treated with tenderness. If she were a man...but then again, if she were a man, I wouldn't be in this predicament."

He and Ewan left and climbed into their carriage. They didn't speak during the ride home.

Eleven

Clarissa looked up from her bookkeeping as Mrs. Lankston, their foolish but kind neighbor, entered the shop. Clarissa exchanged a smile with Gilbert who was engaged in the task of polishing Clarissa's latest acquisition, an authentic silver table arrangement dating from George III's earliest years.

"How do you do, Mrs. Lankston?" He offered a grin.

Did his mood improve a notch at the expectation of an amusing tale to come?

"I have a story today, kith," Mrs. Lankston said.

Clarissa awarded her the smallest beam of pleasure. The red-haired woman glanced from one sibling to the other.

"What is it, madam?" Gilbert inquired.

"You two could be twins."

Gilbert raised a brow.

"No, I tell a lie. You only moderately resemble each other. Your eyes differ."

"Hers are inherited from our papa, Aden. Do you remember him?"

"Yes. He was well esteemed. He always had a cheerful hello. Much grieved for."

"Thank you," Gilbert said. "He was a good man."

"Your mother was quite taken with him. He would look at her with those unusual eyes."

"Rare." Gilbert looked at Clarissa. "She's blessed that they are flattering on a woman as well."

"Exceptionally so."

Clarissa fussed with a short pile of books. "Thank you, but I stood out as a child. Our playmates made me the brunt of whatever game we were playing. They mocked me, calling me odd. Some of them said I scared them when I turned in their direction. They wondered if I had wickedness in me. A girl told me eyes of my shade didn't really exist, that I was born with blue eyes and had them until the devil paid me a visit and our father as well. I'm an oddity."

"Oddity, my dear? You are beautiful."

"You're mistaken, madam. But thank you. I have only had two serious suitors in my life."

"Because your intelligence startles most men! Your papa refused to raise you differently from your brother. People heard you analyzing political issues in conversation. It frightened beef-witted gentlemen away. I am a fan of the unusual, as you can see by a simple stroll through my hat shop. You're a gem, as your brother has called you."

"You're very kind."

"But seeing you two, your affection for each other is encouraging. You appear close."

"We are," Gilbert said.

Clarissa gave him a smile of approval.

"We have been through plenty of hard times together, Mrs. Lankston," he added.

"Mrs. Lankston," Clarissa began, "your story? I, and my brother, anxiously anticipate your words."

"Oh yes." She stepped closer. "Any word on that water clock I wish to acquire?"

"Oh." Clarissa raised her brow.

Mrs. Lankston was hesitating, and to her complete puzzlement, changing the subject.

"Well that order is a little more difficult to procure. Water clocks are ancient."

"You could find them in A.D. thirteen hundred."

"Yes, madam, next we had mechanical clocks."

"Clarissa?" Gilbert asked.

She turned and faced her brother. "It was made in fourteen hundred B.C. It had a clay bowl with dots that marked the hours as water dripped slowly out of the bottom of the bowl. Then it was improved."

"Near four hundred B.C., by the Greeks. They used glass then, and painted the hours on the outside. Those clocks may not have worked well, but they were interesting."

"Most people still liked to use the sun to tell time."

Gilbert raised his brow. "Fascinating, ladies. That was a stunning story..." he trailed off sarcastically.

Clarissa tapped his arm.

"That was not the tale I came to tell." Mrs. Lankston smirked.

He bowed and extended his arms. "Then please, madam."

"I am glad you have a protective brother for times of trouble, my dear lady."

Clarissa pursed her lips.

"It would be difficult for you to tell the time using the sun, now...I mean, as the situation grows darker around you. As you descend into shadow."

Clarissa stared at her, perplexed and mildly alarmed by this nonsense. "But there are sun-dials everywhere."

Gilbert stepped forward, ahead of his sister. "Madam?"

"I saw Mr. Amberley...the charming brother, Duncan, the captain, not that dreadfully rude brother of his," she rattled on. "Once I had the displeasure of crossing paths with the younger brother at the home of a mutual acquaintance. I could not wait to be relieved of his presence. He smirked at me as if I were not worth greeting, because I was not what he would have considered a suitable bedmate. But the captain is a gentleman."

Clarissa touched her chest. "Duncan?"

Gilbert turned to observe her.

"You really love your husband. It shows in your reverence at the mere mention of his name. The word 'Duncan' puts a glow on your face." Mrs. Lankston warmed to her theme. "And you tremble as a velvet rose petal during the dusting of a spring shower would."

"You are a true poet, Mrs. Lankston," Gilbert said.

"Well, thank you." She blushed and fingered her bright purple bonnet. She straightened and cleared her throat. "As I was saying, your husband, Clarissa, the fine man that he is, and so striking!"

Clarissa gave her an exasperated smile.

"Oh, yes. My husband and I, the Reverend Lankston, were on parish duties, and we saw the captain contributing most generously to the sale of work for our more destitute families in the area. A few of those adorable females, I can proudly say, are the beneficiaries of my most unique hats!"

She fluttered her hands. "I saw Mrs. Sheldon wearing a personal favorite of mine, a brightly colored orange bonnet with little gold bells and a lime green feather. Delightful, delightful I tell you!" She frowned thoughtfully. "Though it didn't suit the drab cotton print dress bestowed on her fine womanly figure."

Gilbert and Clarissa gaped at her, speechless.

"Whatever is the matter?" the older lady asked.

Gilbert broke out laughing. "It was the mental picture. Again you entertain us, Mrs. Lankston, thank you for such fine amusement!"

Clarissa couldn't help but chuckle.

Mrs. Lankston frowned. "I wasn't finished with my story, and Mr. Hale, I wasn't intending on an amusing anecdote."

"Accept my apology, madam."

"Yes. Now, my dear." She took Clarissa's hand in hers. "Try not to be sad. It's the talk of the town. People have a theory as to why such a fetching couple lives separately."

"Do you believe this is hurting her reputation, madam?"

"Only the beef-witted say so. The rest wish to understand." She looked back at Clarissa. "There are those who say the younger Mr.

Amberley chased you away with his vile behavior. It's recognized around town what a problem he is. His poor family..."

Clarissa held her tongue.

"Your husband approached us like a true gentleman would, and he made a large order."

"For women's bonnets?" Clarissa asked, surprised.

"Yes."

"Were they for lavender or burgundy? Duncan's mother prefers those colors."

Mrs. Lankston gave her a regretful look. "No. I should not have spoken. Hush my silly mouth."

Clarissa slumped her shoulders.

"Oh, I'm forlorn over this. It never crossed my mind. He said they were for a fashionable young lady who fancies bright copper in particular and that cost wasn't a concern."

"I hate copper, and I once told him that." Clarissa drew a breath in through her nose. "Thank you, Mrs. Lankston."

"Do not repine too much over it. Doubtless there is an explanation. Now, I must be off." She left.

"Busy-body," Gilbert muttered.

Twelve

The towering columns of the home of Gilbert and Clarissa's wealthy client, Mr. Wyndham, appeared at the end of a long drive. The siblings rolled up in their hired cab.

Clarissa teasingly dusted her brother's arm. "I'm gratified you wore Papa's finest velvet suit."

"It's a bit antiquated, but it cost him a pretty packet at the time, well cut from fine cloth. I expect he's having a chuckle, if he can see us from heaven. For a dinner party such as this, I could not arrive in less."

She smiled sadly. "I wish Harriet were here."

"Me too, sister."

"To think, Gilbert, we only obtained this invitation, delivered to the shop, because I was able to procure an old dusty suit of armor for our patron."

"He was amazed, but not me. And he'd been to five other possible suppliers first."

"Yet, I wonder…"

"He has a weakness for showing off his house—bought it from a destitute aristocrat."

"I see no less than fifteen carriages. His enterprises pay enormously well."

Gilbert tapped her arm affectionately then gripped it.

"What is the matter?"

"Nothing. Worry not."

She fidgeted. Duncan's carriage came to her notice, and she drew in a sharp breath. They made their way to the house.

A butler showed them into the front salon where Mr. Wyndham came forward to greet them warmly.

Clarissa curtsied. "Mr. Wyndham, I am encouraged you are so content with my brother and me."

The tall, blond, and handsome well-dressed gentleman bowed slightly to her. His dark coat would have cost far more than the suit of armor he had purchased from Clarissa.

He bowed over Clarissa's fingertips again. "I am pleased you and your brother have accepted my invitation this evening. You have completed a collection for me that has taken fifteen years in its composition."

Gilbert then led her forward, following the butler.

~ * ~

Duncan was positioned ten feet behind Gilbert and Clarissa. He turned to leave, having no intention of being confronted by his wife and her brother, but Mr. Wyndham forestalled him.

"Captain Amberley, I would be offended if you did not stay. I'd appreciate having you here. Contacts and friendship are so necessary in business, is that not true? This night honors those who have done me a service. You brought the finest horses to my stables."

Duncan followed a servant to the drawing room where the guests assembled. Gilbert whispered something into Clarissa's ear. A member of parliament approached them, and Duncan frowned, suspecting something bad.

"What is an MP doing in this kind of company—and how are they acquainted with him in any case?"

Their earnest conversation piqued Duncan's curiosity, and he stepped closer to listen, unseen behind a Greek statue.

The MP shrugged. "Mr. Hale, divorces..."

"And Countess Dalrymple..."

Duncan inhaled slowly. "Dash it!"

A lady approached with her partner. Duncan grumbled in frustration. The MP walked away. Clarissa blinked against sparkling tears. Gilbert took out a handkerchief and dabbed at them.

"It should be me doing that," Duncan muttered.

The guests were in different stages of tipsiness. Behind Duncan came the sounds of two men in their cups laughing. The taller man told his companion a wild tale of a duke in days gone past who accidently married his sister. Too intrigued to move away, Duncan listened.

"He actually—" the speaker interrupted his own story with infectious laughter, "made it to the wedding bed before he recognized her as his sister!"

"How is that possible?" his friend asked.

"Well sir, they had been raised apart. She had been brought up in Italy. The duke had only met her once, a year previously. He had forgotten that because he was drunk at the time. So was she. He saw her once again and was instantly enamored. He sent for her, and being drunk, told her a silly name that his friends called him at the club, like sir stupid or something. Anyway," he said and chuckled, "she agreed to marry him because she was fast becoming a spinster."

"How did they discover the truth before the marriage was consummated?" the gentleman asked.

"He..."

"He what?"

"He saw her necklace, which was in the form of the family emblem. He jumped out of the bed as if he were on fire. She jumped up too, screaming. It was humorous. They woke up the whole household. A maid came in with a bucket of water and splashed the still-drunk duke. He shook like a drowned rat, dumbfounded. Soon the entire town knew of this. The perpetually drunk noble finally tossed out the bottle for good."

They laughed.

"That is the outside of enough!" someone said.

Duncan managed a small smile. He glanced up and saw Gilbert and Clarissa watching the men, gaping.

Later, seated for supper, Clarissa stretched her gaze across the long table. Duncan suspected she saw him for the first time that evening because she suddenly sat back, fidgeting like she did when she felt tension. Her fingertips went to her mouth.

Gilbert tapped her forearm and whispered into her ear. She nodded with new resolve. Duncan stole glances at her during supper. Coffee was served, and he continued to observe her, ignoring his cup.

They rose from the table, and the musicians played. Mr. Wyndham bowed to Clarissa. Duncan cringed and made his way closer to them.

"Miss Hale," their host said.

Duncan opened his mouth to announce that he was mistaken about her name.

"Sir," she said with a coy look. "You have only recently returned from your journey. I have become Mrs. Amberley."

"What?" Mr. Wyndham asked. "Do you refer to Duncan or Ewan? It could not be Duncan because he has been here tonight, but surely you could not mean...Ewan, no, Duncan is the sibling with honor."

"It is Duncan, of course."

Mr. Wyndham inhaled audibly, and his posture stiffened. He scanned the room. "I am at a loss."

Duncan arrived before them.

Their host stared at them, speechless at first. "I am afraid I do not understand. I anticipated calling on Miss Hale, but I see that is impossible. Why have you two not spoken a word to each other this entire evening?"

Regret slumped Duncan's shoulders.

Their host's brow rose. "So that's why my old friend in parliament brought up the subject of...uh...never mind. I think I shall take my leave. You two must talk. I'll wager Ewan has something to do with your troubles." He passed Clarissa over to her husband then walked away.

Duncan lovingly caught a hold of her hands. "Clarissa, I..." his voice caught in his throat.

Her tremble coursed up his arms. He gestured, and she followed him to a quiet, shaded corner near another marble statue.

She frowned. "Why, Duncan?"

"Why what?"

"Why can't I forget the memory of falling into your arms? Why can't I stop loving you?"

"You cannot ignore our marriage."

"You want me to love you still?"

"Yes. I'm obsessed with the color of turquoise stones now."

"You distress me but have given me a gift."

"To what do you refer?"

"I'm better off for having experienced such incredible love. Some never do."

His breath suspended.

"Now that I have had it, though it is lost, I can search for and eventually find peace."

"My love," he uttered.

Her lips tipped into a sad smile. "You wore the jacket."

He touched it. "Yes. It has grown to be my favorite." He remembered the day Clarissa had pointed it out and expressed her appreciation of it, its dark wool, unadorned, but with an exquisite cut. He asked her if he should acquire it. She had told him yes but that he did not need her permission. He had responded that he would not wear it unless he appeared impossibly irresistible to her in it. Her blush told him what he needed to know. How fortunate he had worn it this evening.

He noticed a loose ribbon trailing from her slipper. "Clarissa, allow me." He bent to the floor.

A small gasp escaped her lips as she tossed a glance around.

"I do not wish for you to trip."

As he lifted the hem of her gown an inch, he noticed the slippers had a pattern on them that matched the hem of her dress. Reverently, he tied the delicate ribbon. She flinched as if a current had surged through her. His hand slid to her ankle, and he felt her tremble.

He inched to his feet. "I remember running my fingertips over your ankles, so slowly, higher."

She frowned. "Please stop. I am ill. I must ask Gilbert to escort me away from here."

"Look at me, dear. I want to see your beautiful eyes, for you to see the truth in mine. It's more than desire." He gave her a loving smile. "Tell me again that it's over between us. You cannot, can you?" He spoke against her ear. "Remember when I last had you in my arms, how you responded. I may retire early to spend my days pleasuring you."

"Stop!"

Gilbert approached them. "Clarissa is well, I trust?"

She shook her head.

Gilbert looked at Duncan. "Then, with your permission, I will escort my sister home. She's pale."

Reluctantly, Duncan released her. "If she takes a turn for the worse, you will notify me, Gilbert."

"Of course. She is your wife."

"Yes, she is."

~ * ~

Two days later, informed by a messenger of Clarissa's distress, Duncan pushed through the door of her shop and strode across the creaky floor toward the back of the emporium. He greeted Gilbert quickly and shoved aside the curtain divider, taking the stairs two at a time. He tapped on Clarissa's door.

"Come in." He heard her voice, a soft, sad response.

He opened her door and shut it behind him. She lay on her side, on a couch, facing the opposite wall.

He approached and sat by her recumbent form, placing his hand on her hip. "Clarissa."

"Hello." She shifted. "Why are you here?"

"Because I care for you."

"You'll miss your meeting."

"What meeting?"

"Months ago, you told me about a meeting with horse breeders. You've mentioned it a dozen times and told me to remind you—as if you'd forget. It was really important, you told me. You were hoping to acquire a rare beauty. You made an incredibly high bid. Go, or you stand to lose more money than Gilbert and I could earn in a lifetime."

He frowned. "I don't care."

"What?" Her voice rose in surprise.

"Gilbert said you needed me."

"Please go." Tears rolled down her cheeks.

He dried them with his thumb. "Eat something."

"Is that what this is about?"

"Gilbert informed me you weren't eating. He called me here, anxious. I will not have my wife starve. If your gowns begin to hang on you, I will force you to eat."

"You wouldn't."

"I most certainly would. A humiliating experience, I'd suspect. I would advise you to avoid it."

She sat up. "Very well, I'll eat! I'll gorge myself if it will please you."

"Good." He smiled with relief. "Now prepare to go down to your shop. Your business will suffer without your expertise."

She sighed.

"I still have time for that meeting. You're adorable." He kissed her and left.

~ * ~

Three days later, Clarissa and Gilbert arrived at the asylum in their hired coach. She shuddered, facing the dark, forbidding presence.

Gilbert glanced at Clarissa. "Why won't you tell me what this is about? Why do you and Duncan need to end your marriage? Why won't you tell me the exact reason we spoke to that Member of Parliament concerning your options?"

"Because I fear you'll hate Duncan."

"Why would I? I'm fond of him. Whatever his brother did, your husband is not involved."

"Perhaps so, but he defends his brother."

"Clarissa, elaborate."

"You won't hate Duncan?"

"No."

"Promise?"

"Yes."

She nodded. After she informed her brother about Harriet's abduction, she shifted. He gripped the sides of his seat.

"Gilbert?"

He inhaled deeply. "I had a right to know this. You should have told me in the beginning."

"Forgive me."

He looked at her sternly. "I don't appreciate that you withheld information from me."

"I've defended Harriet since the beginning. I love her and believe her. I lost my husband to defend her. And you said Duncan had integrity, that he had a good reason for his actions."

"I did."

"Did you mean it?"

"Yes. I forgive you. Let's procure the evidence we will need to expose Ewan. Then you can go and comfort your scandalized husband. You can forgive him, can you not?"

"Yes. He believes his brother is innocent."

"Then I can forgive Duncan too."

They walked inside and searched out the doctor, turning down grim halls. Clarissa bit her lip and felt the flush of uneasiness as they passed through the bleak building. An attendant led them to the doctor, a well-dressed, polite man of middling years, gray dusting his dark hair. During the interview, the doctor treated them with respect and gave his answers in a friendly, professional fashion. An hour later, Clarissa and Gilbert came out, frowning.

"Mr. Amberley's story is confirmed. The doctor remembers Harriet—as a patient here, even described her." He gave his sister a savage look. "It's a lie, I tell you!"

"That place was horrible. I don't care what the doctor said. I believe Harriet."

"Thank you." He tapped his walking stick on the ground with force. "We'll prove her right, even if we become street beggars in the process. We have to take up this matter ourselves, gathering proof at least."

"It may ruin us financially, but that's not the most important issue."

"My wife comes first."

"Yes, but we will find a way not to lose our family legacy, I do hope."

"Yes, Clarissa. We can do this."

"We *will* do this."

"I see your sadness and can guess your mind has turned to your husband. Do not give up hope. Duncan loves you."

"I'm disappointed he chose his brother over me, but..."

He turned to her before the hired carriage and wrapped his hands around hers. "Now wait a minute. I've been pondering this, and it isn't fair. You chose Harriet over him."

"Let's not discuss this now."

"All right."

~ * ~

That night, Clarissa spent hours in private conversation with Harriet in Clarissa's entrance room, trying to get clues to this mystery. Her future happiness depended on her finding a happy solution for everyone involved. Harriet cried on Clarissa's shoulder.

Clarissa stroked her hair. "My poor Harriet."

"I use my left hand to paint though I use my right for everything else because when he had me chained to that bed, I strained my right wrist trying to get free. He brought me paper and watercolors in an attempt to appease me. I had to paint with my left hand and grew accustomed to it."

"Have you told me all?"

"Yes, except..."

Clarissa shifted.

"I recall he violated me, doing things to me."

At the horror of it, Clarissa's composure evaporated.

"But oddly, he took the time to pleasure me against my will, and taught me things, though I didn't aspire to learn."

Clarissa swallowed down her nausea.

"I believe he has a birthmark, or it's probably a scar."

"Where?" she uttered.

"Right below his...trouser line, where a woman would see."

"Elaborate."

"I was so confused, so terrified, but I think I saw it. It's a red scar."

I must see for myself, then go to Duncan. It will prove beyond a doubt that his brother is guilty. I will apologize and comfort him. We will get through it together.

She clenched her jaw, thinking Duncan would initially be shocked finding her with his brother but when she explained her evidence, he would understand, she knew.

"I wish we could discover that it wasn't simply my imagination and go straight to Duncan with the evidence."

"Mr. Amberley finds me...attractive."

"What are you thinking?"

Clarissa coaxed Harriet gently back onto her shoulder. "Don't you worry." Clarissa kissed her cheek and went downstairs.

The next day she detected a dusty box in the storeroom of the emporium and removed the tarty clothes from within. The costume for a fancy dress party would serve her purpose. She slipped each article of clothing on while seething with anger then regarded her strumpet appearance in a mirror lying against the dark wall.

"Hm, I appear a light-skirt, or a theatre dancer. He should appreciate that." Disgusted with herself but determined, she put a heavy, concealing coat over her attire. She went outside, finding a hackney cab.

During the ride to Amberley, as the cab climbed the steep streets toward the large country house in Hampstead, she wavered between fear and anger, her lips clasped tight one moment, butterflies in her stomach the next. She focused on the clippity-clop of the horses' hooves, but it didn't help, so she chose to feed her anger in order to gear up for the distasteful task ahead.

It being evening, right after supper, she planned to go around to her brother-in-law's wing of the house, an area she had not once seen, even when she resided on the premises. He had parties and women, and knew this often annoyed his brother, so he stayed in the most private area where he wouldn't be bothered.

Too bad he had to dine with us so often, she recalled.

Clarissa had the hackney driver drop her near Whitestone Pond. She looked to the left. A large, white weatherboard building loomed there. The right afforded a person a wonderful view of London. She turned and spotted her husband's grand home and slipped onto the grounds unnoticed. Slinking around to Mr. Amberley's section, she inhaled deliberately and peeked into a window. She tapped on it, mortified, but not relishing being discovered by a servant. Duncan's brother came to the window, gaping. She pressed a finger to her lips then gestured toward a door on the side of the house. Anger, fear, shame, and excitement mingled in her blood, and quick feet brought her to that door.

A surprised Mr. Amberley opened the door. After his look of shock faded, he eyed her with lust. "Clarissa?" he asked with a narrowed brow. "Why are you here?"

"Does it matter?" She flirted with him under lowered lids.

"You're enchanting."

Her fists rested at her sides. "Damn him."

"Who?"

"Duncan."

"Ah."

She tipped her head sideways, flirtatiously. "Can I have a word with you? I wish for a bit of retribution against my husband."

He eyed her with suspicion. "But you think me a criminal."

"I have recently uncovered evidence to the contrary."

"Well, come in." His shoulders lowered a fraction.

She stepped past him. He shut the door.

Once inside, she stood close to him. He lifted the back of his fingers to her hair. It was arranged in curls on her shoulders this evening, inviting, like she had intended.

Thirteen

Clarissa's brother-in-law waited in the front entrance of his private rooms in their home.

"Mr. Amberley, this has gone too far. Let's put our cards on the table. I went to the asylum and spoke with Dr. Dearborn. He confirmed your story. I have no choice but to believe you," she fibbed.

"Excellent." His bright smile could have rendered her sightless.

She looked down with feigned coyness. "I'm so disappointed in Duncan. I'm angry he didn't defend me. I want to...punish him." She glanced back up and gulped down her revulsion. "Do you find me... comely?"

"Is this what I think it is?"

"Yes."

"Would you consider a little game of charades? Feign being my wife tonight. That will show my arrogant brother." He leered. "When he was courting you, I told him I could charm you away from him. A single night with me will prove it."

She ran a finger down his chest. "You're handsome."

He reached for her.

She backed away. "There is one thing."

He stepped to her and stroked her cheek. "What?"

"Could we go to a private little area a ways behind the stables? Duncan and I have amused ourselves there as a thrill. What better area to compare brothers?" She swallowed the queasiness that threatened to destroy her plan.

"A fine idea!"

They walked to their destination, circled to the back of the stables, and kept going. She paused near an oak and lit the hanging lantern. He bent to kiss her. Clarissa calculated the time. She knew that Duncan, at this time, at the end of each week, went for a stroll and passed this spot with regularity.

She was taking a terrible chance. Mr. Amberley grabbed her arms and covered her mouth with his. Her spine stiffened. It was not Duncan's kiss, and disgust burned in her chest. She forced her tears back and helped Mr. Amberley off with his shirt. It crumpled to the ground. He kissed her again.

Dreadful ardor filled his moves and made her shiver.

"You're so beautiful. If I get you with child, I may even do the honorable thing."

Clarissa swallowed hard, looking into his wickedly handsome green eyes. "I am already Duncan's wife."

"If you could put that deeply happy look on my face that I saw on my brother's, then you will banish thoughts of him. I could take my portion of the inheritance and bear you away. Where I took you, no one would have to be privy to the fact that you were already married."

"You would be a party to bigamy...your own brother...you could do that to him and to me? Break the sacred vows of matrimony."

"If you could put that expression on my face, Clarissa, yes. He was given the lot of it, nothing spared. I was given naught in comparison. Yes, I would take from him the solitary thing he would have given it all for."

"He would have given up everything for me?"

"He has told me so. It's most unfortunate that his behavior proved this to be a lie. This will be a sweet night. You will have your revenge against a husband who did not champion you."

"Does he not do so for your sake? Do you really wish to do this to him?"

He shifted uncomfortably. "When I have such a beautiful woman here, and I am preparing to make love to her, I don't concern myself with such things."

Clarissa bit her lip. If Duncan didn't show up, there was her other idea, slipping the sleeping tablet into Mr. Amberley's mouth and telling him an apothecary assured her it enhanced pleasure, but that was riskier than this.

His eyes sparkled under the light of a full moon and the yellow circle cast by the lantern. He slipped his inexpressibles down past his hips. A jagged red birthmark or scar cut across his skin.

A man gasped.

Duncan!

She spun to face him. He was gaping, an expression of horror on his face. Mr. Amberley pulled up his drawers.

"Duncan, Duncan, his scar! Harriet told me about it. She didn't lie!"

Duncan stumbled.

"Damn you, Clarissa." Mr. Amberley shoved her.

She fell back and hit her head on the tree. Her world went black.

~ * ~

Ewan ran.

"Ewan, damn you!"

Duncan turned and saw his wife sprawled on the ground. Her eyes were closed, and she didn't move. A rock rested by her foot. Trembling, he bent and placed his ear against her chest, listening for a heartbeat. Relieved, he picked her up and glanced at his house, in the direction of Ewan's rooms, tasting bile.

He rushed Clarissa inside. After he gently laid her on his bed, he sent servants for the doctor and to inform her brother of the situation.

Later, Duncan clasped Clarissa's limp hand as the doctor closed up his bag.

"Doctor?"

"A head injury. She could have died. Watch that laceration near her brow."

"Will she wake up?"

"I believe so."

~ * ~

Duncan looked after the sleeping Clarissa. She grew feverish. He dozed restlessly beside her.

One night, she mumbled. "Harriet, I will have to seduce his brother. I must find out."

Duncan bolted upright from his resting position, tortured with agony and betrayal. The next day, the spoon quivered as he fed her. He was so angry with Ewan he refused to speak to him, prepared to have him banished from the house. His mother stopped him with her pleas.

Two days later, Clarissa sat up, her cheeks pink after days of being pale. "Go and see your brother. Tell him to show you the scar. Insist he lower his…"

"Trousers?" At her words, the pain of doubt and loss made him shake with revulsion. "I will not. Why were you with him in that compromising situation? You lured him there, did you not? Your clothes say you did." He watched her through angry tears.

"He tried to kill me."

Gripping the armrests of a chair close to the bed, he scoffed. "You slipped on a rock, and after I discovered you there together."

"I'm fine now, but I almost died for this. Go, Duncan."

"You appear to have recovered well, and I'm glad for it. Would you now kindly leave my home?"

"Duncan," she cried, "I'm in love with you. Don't make me leave. This is my home, with you."

"You are a harlot."

She reached for his hand, but he drew it away.

"No, I had to see. We didn't do anything. I wouldn't. Harriet described the scar, when your brother forced himself on her. I was only after evidence."

He thrust a finger at her. "Now your story gets elaborate. Clever, Clarissa." He smirked. "You discovered a so-called scar and thought fast—say your sister-in-law gave you this information. I have always thought you were intelligent. This proves it."

She swung her legs around and slapped her feet to the floor. "If I wanted him, why would I be saying these things to you now?"

He shrugged. "Fear?"

She twisted the bed cover. "I beg you. Go and ask Harriet, before I have a chance to talk to her. Ask her about the scar. You will see I'm telling the truth."

His brow narrowed. "It would be deeply inappropriate for me to have such a conversation with Mrs. Hale."

"I care no longer if you defend your brother's life. In fact, it's admirable of you to do so, but please, Duncan, let me be your wife again, even as I defend my sister! You cared for me these past days. It felt right being in your arms." Her hands came up, and then she slapped them down, onto her lap. "I missed you so much." She sobbed, stood, and wrapped her arms around him.

He pushed her away gently. "Go home. Infidelity could get me a divorce now."

"Will you continue to side with him still?"

Vexed, he grasped his forearm. "Because he's not a killer! I will not see my brother hanged, but he'll get a sound thrashing in a boxing salon as I get my retribution."

"I beg you, believe me. I want to stay with you!"

"No! I keep imagining you two by that tree, where you and I made love. Then a few days ago, he was half-nude, standing there with you."

"He tripped me. He is capable of murder and tried to kill me!" Her face flushed.

He waved her away. "It's time for you to take your leave."

"I promise you, I'm not lying!" Tears rolled down her cheeks. "I will prove my innocence. I wouldn't have demeaned myself with him. I was expecting you. Remember your regular strolls there at that time? If you hadn't come, I would have put him to sleep with—"

"Drop this case," he challenged.

"He killed a woman by accident. Maybe the jury will spare him, but he deeply wronged my sister."

"Leave," he said calmly. "I'll have Phineas drive you home."

"Why don't you love me?" She left sobbing.

Duncan scrutinized her from his window. "You're wrong," he whispered with bitterness to the empty room. "If I'm furious it's because I'm so in love with you." He went to see his coachman.

Fourteen

Bandaged up on his arms and sides, Ewan reclined on a Grecian couch in the yellow drawing room. He held a cold cloth to his eye. Moving an inch caused him to cringe. He spoke through swollen lips. "You nearly killed me, Duncan."

Duncan bristled in a mahogany Trafalgar chair beside him. "Quite right! You dared to touch my wife," he grumbled. "If you were not my brother, I would have been in Newgate, awaiting a hanging for murder."

"I daresay the beating was worth it."

Duncan lunged out of his chair and paced over the carpeted floor, his fists clenched as he glared at Ewan. "I am more than half disposed to send you away, far away, and settle an allowance on you because it would content our mother to give you the money. The only thing that stops me is the investigation in which we are currently engaged and our mother's pleading to forgive you." He bent close to Ewan. "I've a dashed good mind to do it anyway."

Ewan shot up a weak hand. "Pray do not strike me again. Permit me to recover before you beat me again, else I own you will be responsible for my death. Explain that to our mother."

Duncan sat, resigned. He put his elbows on his knees and rubbed his cheeks. "Why have you done this to me? I'm in love with her." He gripped Ewan's forearms.

"You suspect why," Ewan managed.

"The devil I do!"

"Do you remember us as young cubs? You had finished your studies young."

The marquetry clock flanked by two candelabra on the mantelpiece chimed out the quarter hour.

Duncan glanced at it and back at Ewan. "It wasn't easy being the junior of my classmates. I worked hard, doubling up my classes."

"Yes, yes, my great older brother, the great Duncan. You were not yet a man..." he struggled. "...when you joined the Navy. Do you remember what happened shortly before you stepped onto your first ship?"

Duncan's breaths rushed out. "Yes?"

"That girl you were calling on?"

"Catherine," he uttered.

"Yes, Catherine. She was a beauty. I wanted her, Duncan. I came across her first. She batted her eyelashes at me."

"And?"

"After weeks of playing her coy games, she accepted me. Then you walked past, wearing your uniform, and she forgot about me."

"I left two weeks later."

"She cried over you, on my shoulder!" He coughed.

Duncan was stunned into silence.

"And she was not the only one. Every girl I ever danced attendance upon who saw you or your portrait asked me about you, dash it! Not our other brothers. You!"

Duncan shook his head.

"The girls craved more information on you," Ewan continued. "I swore I would take a woman from you. I would take *the* woman."

Duncan grasped his knees, his gut tight with anger.

"Damn, did fortune strike me? Not only did you fall passionately in love, but she was a woman I lusted after. You may have had her first, but I had her last."

Duncan shuddered. His brother's voice sent quakes through him.

"She wanted to compare brothers. That's what she told me. Do you wonder how you compared to me? Maybe I'll tell you what she said, but then again, maybe I won't. Maybe she now carries my child."

Duncan's fury called to be unleashed. He drew on his discipline as a naval captain in order not to strike Ewan dead. He shoved his finger at him. "You mustn't on any account show yourself to me until I deign to allow it." With the contained wrath of a simmering volcano, he bounded to his feet and left his brother's ugly presence. He would not look at him until he trusted himself not to injure him further.

Duncan worked days without much rest. After the seventh, a tap sounded at his office door. The door came open, and his mother, Evina, greeted him. She tucked a stray brown curl into her bonnet. Duncan noted her traditional Scottish plaid draped over the shoulder of her English walking dress.

"Come in." He got to his feet.

She walked in and sat across from him. He resumed his seat.

She reached across his desk for him. "What would I do without you? Ewan tries me." She still had a slight Scottish brogue after these passing years, and her smooth voice gave Duncan comfort.

"He tries all of us."

"Aye, yet he's still my child. Think you I have not spent overlong..." Her voice drifted.

"Do not worry. I look out for him, even the times I want to kill him."

"You might have killed him."

"No. I have restraint and foresight, even in the midst of fury, and can stop in time."

"Yes, you do. He deserved it for hurting you so, but thank you for controlling yourself. He's full of folly and has embarrassed our family beyond bearing oftimes. Another mother might have asked him to withdraw himself from under our roof. But I must forgive him. Nothing else is possible."

He wanted to reassure her the way she did him when his brothers died. "I will honor your wishes."

"I'm wretched for your suffering. I love you. You are the joy of my life. You suffer your brother's actions to honor my wishes to help him. Thank you."

He nodded. She stood, and so did he.

She walked around his desk and hugged him. "Duncan?" She gave his hands a squeeze then let hers rest at her sides.

"Yes?"

"Your brother-in-law—"

"Gilbert."

"Yes. Clarissa informed me of a conversation she had with him the day of your introduction."

"Oh?" He raised his brow in his interest.

"They called you a hero. It's obvious even to virtual strangers that you are such a man. Clarissa also said that on that day, she chanced upon the man she wanted to spend her life with. I believe her. I do not understand what happened behind the stables, but I am convinced she loves you."

"How can you be sure?"

"Clarissa has had discussions with me when you were engaged with work or otherwise occupied. She's in love with you. I am lost as to why she did what she did, but do not give up on your happiness. There's more to the matter than is obvious."

Hope sprang forth. "What else has she said to you?"

"I had to avert her once from…"

"From what?"

"She was going to give her half of the shop to her brother, so she could dedicate her time to you."

"That place is her purpose in life."

She smiled. "Yet she prepared to give it up thinking it would please you. I stopped her."

"I'm glad you did. It was her father's dream to make the family business successful, and now it is her dream and Gilbert's."

"I knew you would want me to prevent her from letting that dream go." She hugged him, and then left the office.

Duncan stared at the closed door. He had a serious decision to make.

Fifteen

Weeks after his fight with Ewan, Duncan was able to shut the image of his brother's beaten body out of his mind long enough to go to his club in Pall Mall Street, 'The Naval Retreat,' an elegant Georgian house. Walking under arcade-like windows filling up the inner-columns, he glanced up at the naval symbols and weapons decorating their arches.

After signing in under the light of a crystal chandelier made of the finest glass, he scanned the room for his friend. When his tall, light-haired associate, the baronet Sir Roger Brittingham came into view, he inclined his head in greeting. Duncan smiled, amused, thinking of Brittingham's passion to drive his equipage like a madman and consort with opera dancers. Brittingham could be counted on for the sheer entertainment of his reckless antics. He was currently yards away from a portrait of his staider sire. The picture hung among those of other previous members, decorating the silk wallpaper. Brittingham's parent would lecture him on his drinking and gambling habits if he were alive.

"Captain," Brittingham addressed Duncan with the term he was fond of for him.

Duncan glanced at him and steered him past the smoking room. "What, no jokes today?"

Brittingham peered into the billiards room. "The table's vacant, and I will spare you a ribbing today. Though, you would be even further advanced by now if—"

Duncan shot him a warning look. "I put England first, but those Americans I sent off my ship were innocent. A person has to have honor. Besides, I had to come home and run the estate."

"Well, Captain, fancy a fencing match soon? It's been too long since I last humiliated you," Brittingham quipped.

"You humiliated me?" Duncan laughed. "It seems you are in your cups again, my friend."

"The day is young. Perchance later." He glanced at the uniformed servants moving about the room and gestured to a footman who approached. "Bring us a bottle of that excellent brandy I had last week."

"Yes, sir."

"You best not drink too much, or you risk embarrassing yourself. We'll fence soon."

"Capital! A visit to the card rooms as well, or the smoking rooms?"

"Cards. Later. I find smoking not to my liking," Duncan said.

"Here comes old Bantersteel. Earned his fortune in trade. Acts like an aristocrat."

"He's outrageous. I wonder if he'll harass us until we bet on another of his ridiculous antics," Duncan said.

Brittingham chuckled. "I hope so. I nearly split my sides after the last two."

Duncan snickered. "Wagering on who could thrash their carriage faster down a rutted road was entertaining. Seeing that wheel fly off was startling. Thank God our old friend wasn't killed as his carriage turned over."

"I was amused by the last wager." Brittingham grinned.

"You mean whether a certain viscount would be elegantly dressed for his second meeting with Beau Brummel or still wearing one of his outdated, brightly-colored satin suits."

"Bantersteel lost a thousand guineas on that beauty of a wager, betting the viscount would impress Brummel for the meeting."

They laughed.

"Hello, my friends," the short, red-haired man said.

"Banty," Duncan responded.

Brittingham tipped his head in greeting. "Who's up for a wager?"

Duncan gestured. "What is it?"

"Well, Captain," Bantersteel began, "I'll gamble you both five hundred guineas each that Lord Blackmeyer will offer for Miss Belinda Suthersby ahead of spring producing its first flowers."

"I'll take that wager." Brittingham clucked his tongue.

"And you, Captain?"

"No, I fear I cannot accept it."

"Why not?"

"He's not in love," Duncan said. "I saw him the other night consorting with a Bird of Paradise after the opera."

The two gentlemen looked at him as if he were stupid.

"So? What difference does that make?" Bantersteel asked. "He wants Miss Suthersby for her high-born family connections."

"I would normally agree with you, but I've spoken with him. He told me things I'm not at liberty to discuss," Duncan said.

They gave him raised-brow looks, smirking. Bantersteel shook his head.

Another hour or so passed with light-hearted talk, then Duncan caught a snatch of conversation from a couple of men standing nearby in the busy room. He edged nearer, positioning himself inconspicuously close, and sat at a small table, his drink held lingeringly by the side of his face in order to conceal who he was. Two gentlemen were so engrossed in conversation they did not notice him.

"Grey, I tell you, it's true."

"No, a woman with shining blue-green eyes, the color of a turquoise stone?"

"Yes. In Oxford Street. I passed this little emporium with books as well as other items. I went inside because it was my mother's birthday, and I wanted to purchase a gift for her."

"And?" His companion leaned closer.

"In the back of the shop, the loveliest creature I have ever seen turned to me."

Duncan cringed with jealousy, remembering the first time he'd seen her face. He had been seized with an almost animal passion and wanted to take Clarissa right then and there. After that, he'd been to her shop, and she lifted those eyes to him. He had fantasized about putting her down on her counter, lowering himself over her, and kissing her with abandon. He mentally shook off the image.

"And Grey, I would have proposed to her an arrangement as my mistress, but she wore a wedding ring."

"Such a thing doesn't always matter. Many married women are untrue. They are not to be trusted. Maybe you and this beauty still could..." his words dropped off.

Duncan swiped up his coat on the way out. He walked the streets of London until dawn, his thoughts racing, trying to put the pieces together. His brother, his wife, Mrs. Hale, someone was lying. He had assumed it was Mrs. Hale, or rather, that she didn't intentionally lie but was ill. But Clarissa? Ewan had arrogantly told Duncan he had enjoyed her favors, and it only took a few sweet words and a kiss to persuade her. For that, the remnants of his beating lasted a couple of weeks.

The following morning, exhausted and unshaven, Duncan went to Clarissa's shop. She smiled.

"I question why I'm here, Clarissa. But I have an enquiry for you."

"Yes?"

"Which excited you more? When you promised in front of God and witnesses that you would have me as your wedded husband, and I promised to have you..."

She reached for his arm, and he backed away. "Or when you saw my brother unclothed? When I slipped that ring on your finger or when he slipped off your gown?"

"I am, at all times have been, and forever will be your faithful wife. He's lying to you, Duncan. Maybe he continues to lie to keep us at odds, so you won't side with me concerning Harriet."

Disappointment mixed with confusion. He was gladdened by the conviction he saw. The door jingled, and an impoverished ex-army man of good birth, Duncan's private investigator, entered the shop. "Captain Amberley." He glanced at Clarissa.

The man looked at Duncan again. "I've been trying to find you for hours. I went to your home, your club, and your favorite haunts first. Then I figured you had to be here, or at least someone here would be informed of your whereabouts. I have a message for you." He shoved a paper his way.

Duncan scanned it. "Does my brother have this information?"

"No, sir."

"Let me inform him. Pray, keep your silence, and I will double your money."

"Yes, sir." He left.

Duncan whirled to Clarissa. "Darling," he said sarcastically, "this is evidence that your sister-in-law—"

"Harriet...what?"

"She spied briefly for Napoleon during the period she was supposedly missing."

"What?" she shouted. "Give me that!" She grabbed it and read it.

"Now you, my dear, understand what it is like to have a sibling at risk of execution."

"No, no, this has to be a mistake!"

"You have an excellent grasp of the French language. This was taken from an officer of Napoleon. It is a directive to Mrs. Harriet Hale! Maybe they beat her real name from her."

"Oh my God!" Clarissa grew pale. She stumbled. Duncan grasped her arm to prevent her from falling.

"It seems Ewan is not a liar, Clarissa. I figure Napoleon discharged Mrs. Hale after her service to France. Someone saw her wandering, abandoned, and brought her to that asylum." His mouth firmed in disgust.

"Must you report this?"

He stared at her. "No."

She tried to embrace him. He pushed her away without undue force.

"Duncan, please, you must believe me."

"No. You and Ewan..."

"It was nothing. I was trying to get evidence."

"He says you were lovers."

"He's lying."

"He is not!" Duncan shook the papers in her face. Without another word, he stormed out.

~ * ~

That night, Clarissa paced her room, thinking aloud. "What do I hope to gain? But I must pay him a visit!" She lifted her chin, determined, picked up her coat, and slipped it on while descending the stairs to the shop.

At length, she stepped out of the hired cab in front of the Amberley estate and crunched over gravel toward the front door. She climbed the front steps, cast in shadows by lantern light, and shivered. What she was making ready to do... She knocked. The butler, Mr. Dern, bowed, and she followed him in.

"Good evening, Mrs. Amberley."

"Good evening. I'm here to see my husband."

"I shall inform him you are here."

"Thank you."

He walked across the foyer and turned. Moments later, he returned. "He will see you in his office."

She went there, standing at the threshold of the open door.

Duncan scowled. "Why are you here?"

She stepped into his darkly masculine den. Concern for him rushed her. "I was furious with you for choosing to stand by your brother over me. Then Gilbert told me that wasn't a fair thing to do. He is right." She took a step forward, pausing and watching his expression. He frowned.

"I longed for you. When I almost died...you took care of me. I knew I couldn't live without you."

He put down his quill.

"We shouldn't let our families keep us apart. We can remain loyal to them and live together as man and wife. I have learned so much. We don't have to agree on everything."

He curled and uncurled his fingers. "One thing we do have to agree on, Clarissa, is fidelity."

"Duncan." She approached his desk and caressed his arm.

He flinched, and she withdrew her fingers.

"That is true. You are precious to me." She rolled back on her heels, remembering something. "Tell me, who were the copper bonnets for?"

"Mrs. Lankston said something?"

"Yes, I'm afraid so."

"Prinnie asked me to get them for him, to be discreet. They were for a woman he cares for."

Clarissa's lips parted. "You call the Prince Regent Prinnie? There are stories of his close friends doing that."

"No, not to his face. As of yet I haven't earned the right to call him a close friend, though I have done several favors for him. He realizes I have connections his aristocratic friends do not and respects my work in the Navy so at times comes to me, even for mundane things." He went to stand next to her.

"I knew you wouldn't keep a mistress." She cupped his cheek.

He stepped back. "You kept a lover!"

"No, I did not! We have a mystery to solve. I still believe Harriet. She swears she saw your brother accidentally kill that girl. Something else happened as well. We must get to the bottom of things."

"You would take my sibling from me even after I would spare yours."

"Killing and abduction are different than espionage, and I'm not even sure the papers aren't a forgery."

"Her treason disgusts me, offends my loyalties."

"It must be a mistake." She fidgeted with a blue-green ribbon hanging from her gown.

"So must the story of that girl being killed by Ewan."

"Duncan, I don't want to fight with you. When this mystery is solved, whatever the outcome, I want to be your wife."

"You still intend to denounce Ewan. Why? To avenge yourself? Was it he who ended your liaison?"

"No love affair ever existed!" She seized his arm, lowering her voice. "I fear for my life."

"What?" he snapped.

"He tried to kill me. I fear he might attempt to again when he discovers I'm still trying to convict him."

"He did not try to kill you. You tripped."

"He shoved me."

Duncan scoffed. "Answer this, Clarissa. If I had not arrived when I did—"

"I had a secondary plan. An oddity I have in my shop is a package of sleeping pellets from an apothecary. He acquired them from the Far East and gave them to me for a fair price and a book he wanted. I would have given your brother the tablet, lying about what it was, enticing him to take it with a falsehood. The apothecary assured me the effects come quickly."

"That might not have worked!"

"I desperately hoped and expected you'd be there. If both plans failed, I would have fought him, screaming for your servants. If I weren't so desperate to help Harriet, I would never have done something so foolish."

"I wish I could believe you, but Ewan swears you were lovers."

"First of all, it's a question of his arrogant pride. He wants to prove he could get any woman you could, and secondly, he's trying to ruin me, kill me, actually."

"Stop saying that!"

"If I die suddenly, will you be convinced?"

"You're being too dramatic."

"I'm really frightened." Her lower lip quivered.

He stroked her shoulder. "Come now. Don't agitate yourself."

"Could I stay here, under your protection?"

"So near to him."

She bristled, frustrated. "Very well. The future will prove I'm not lying. You'll get your proof. If I make it out of this alive." She hurried away.

~ * ~

Duncan went for his evening stroll with his new puppy, an Old English Sheep dog, in deep thought. The dog barked and ran toward the oak. *That damn oak.* He cringed. His dog sniffed and scratched at the ground. Duncan crouched down to have a look. Something small and white lay there. A pellet! He picked it up. The dog licked up the pellet.

"No, no boy!" He reached in the puppy's mouth, but it was too late.

Concerned, he led the dog to his carriage and hurried to the doctor's house. By the time he arrived, his pet was not moving. He hovered over him as the doctor examined his little friend.

The doctor, a friendly, balding man who wore spectacles, smiled. "Well, Mr. Amberley, it makes a change to look at a canine patient. He'll be fine. He's only asleep."

"Asleep?" he asked.

"Yes. But bring him back if he seems ill when he wakes up. However, I doubt you'll need to."

"Th...thank you," he said with growing certainty as he carried the little animal back to the carriage, cradling his warm body on the way home. By the time they rolled to a stop outside his house, the puppy still hadn't stirred.

The next day, his pet well, he decided to see Clarissa at her home. He wanted to apologize. He entered the Hale shop.

Beneath furrowed brows, unmistakable fear glimmered in Gilbert's face. "Tell me she stayed with you last night, Duncan!"

"What? No! What do you mean?"

"Clarissa wanted to attempt a reconciliation with you. Where is she?"

Duncan led him outside. "We're going to my house. Ewan might have information."

"Ewan, why?"

"Come along!"

"You did reconcile!"

"No."

Gilbert's features drew into a confused scowl. After he locked up, they climbed into the carriage and proceeded to the Amberley home. Duncan neared the house, hopped down from the carriage, and banged on Ewan's door. Ewan opened it, scratching his jaw. Duncan lifted him off the ground six inches by the velvet collar of his coat.

"Where...is...my...wife?" He enunciated each word independently and angrily.

Sixteen

At the outside entrance to his rooms, Ewan gaped, squirming in Duncan's grasp. "Your wife? Of course I'm uninformed of her whereabouts! You two are reconciled then?"

"No!" He released his hold on Ewan and shoved him.

Ewan fell against the doorframe with a thump, wincing, then stumbled outside. Duncan tossed a glance at Gilbert who was leaning on his walking stick beside the carriage. Gilbert shivered in the wintry air. Duncan took a step toward Ewan. Ewan swung his fist at his jaw, but Duncan swerved out of the way then flinched as his brother's booted foot smashed into his shin. With a yell, he grabbed Ewan by the arms and threw him to the ground. He dived down after him, and fists flew as they tussled with shouts of anger.

When blood ran down Ewan's cheek, and his eye swelled closed, Duncan stopped. "You hurt her, didn't you? Hurt my wife." He plopped onto the ground, bending his knees.

"No, I did not hurt her." Ewan scrambled to his feet, grimacing. "I'm leaving."

"I will discover the truth," Duncan promised.

Ewan darted inside the house.

Duncan and Gilbert followed him, their heels clicking over polished wood, and observed as Ewan threw clothes into a portmanteau.

"Clarissa was telling the truth. Admit it. I've unearthed evidence."

"Now what evidence could that be?" Ewan grasped the bag.

"You two were never lovers."

"I swear she came to my door, led me to behind the stables, and was in the process of seducing me!" Ewan made a pleading gesture.

Gilbert gasped and leapt forward, his walking stick thumping on the floor. "That's a lie! Clarissa adores Duncan!"

Ewan shot an arm up against Gilbert's possible attack with his cane—which was not forthcoming. "I am not lying. She wanted to punish him for not defending her."

"So, in a fit she rushed right to you in the name of revenge? Is that what you're saying, Ewan?" Duncan asked.

"Yes! I mean no, I mean—"

Duncan's hands curled into fists. "If that is the truth, then the night I caught you was the first for you two, and I stopped it in time from happening." His shoulders drooped. "I have watched out for you since we were young pups, Ewan. Do you want to deal me a deathblow? You might as well point a pistol at me and shoot." In need of support, he glanced at Gilbert.

Gilbert gave him a stricken glance. Ewan walked toward the door. He exited the house, his feet crunching on the graveled road dotted with clumps of snow then strode off in the direction of the stables.

"You let him leave." Gilbert took a step to follow.

"I'm acquainted with his favorite haunts, but he'll be back. He can't survive on his own."

A hack drew to a stop outside the house.

"I wonder who has come." Gilbert squinted, studying the vehicle.

The coachman let down the steps, and a nervous Mrs. Hale emerged, tipping him a few coins. Gilbert paled. "She never leaves home to go anywhere alone."

Mrs. Lankston waved from the window. Gilbert hurried over to his wife as fast as his lame leg would take him.

Obviously nervous, Mrs. Hale grasped her husband's hand, glancing round. Stray blonde curls framed her red cheeks. "Is *he* here?"

Duncan frowned.

Gilbert wrapped his arm around his wife's shoulders. "My love, what's happened?"

"I came here because I saw you two leave, heard you say where you were going. There's something I must tell you. I came as soon as I could. Mrs. Lankston agreed to accompany me."

Gilbert kissed her cheek. "It was risky to come, darling. Ewan might have been here. You've missed him as it turns out. What is your message?"

"A group of militia men brought Clarissa home minutes after you left."

Duncan gasped. "Clarissa is back?"

"Oh, thank God." Gilbert clutched his chest.

"Mrs. Hale, what happened to my wife?"

"She was distraught, not in her right mind. I begged her to reconsider, but she went in search of evidence of the dead girl. The militia men found her collapsed in an alley by West India dock, under her thick cloak."

Duncan stared at her in disbelief. "She went to the docks? Is she mad?"

"She brought a pistol. We have access to many things through our shop's providers."

Duncan's eyes widened. "Is she hurt?"

"She's uninjured."

"A miracle! I must go to her."

Mrs. Hale approached Mrs. Lankston. "Come with us."

Gilbert offered the older woman help to descend then sent the driver of the hack away.

Mrs. Lankston shifted her violet bonnet with gloved hands then tucked an errant red curl into it. "Thank you." She glanced at Gilbert.

The coachman flipped the reins and was off.

Duncan, Gilbert, and the ladies made their way to Duncan's coach house. Duncan gave instructions to his coachman to drive to the Hale Emporium, then he and the others climbed into his vehicle. They sat on the plush velvet seats.

Mrs. Hale twisted the ties of her reticule. Duncan barely noticed the passing landscape as it blurred by, fists in his lap. As they happened by a main road, the coachman slowed his horses. Carriages crowded the way. There had been an accident.

Duncan slapped his thigh. "I must reach Clarissa!"

They drew closer.

"I recognize that overturned carriage. It's Ewan's!" He threw open the door of his coach, leaped down onto the road, and ran toward Ewan's vehicle. He found Ewan on the ground, grasping his bloodied legs, his face twisted in agony.

Guilt pierced Duncan. "I'm sorry I blamed you for Clarissa's disappearance. I believe you haven't hurt her." He inserted a shoulder beneath Ewan's arm and half carried, half dragged him toward his carriage.

Gilbert and the ladies stepped out of the coach. "We'll find our way from here." He glared at Ewan.

Duncan ordered the driver to take him and his brother to the physician. Once there Duncan spoke with the doctor who told him Ewan must stay bedridden for the time being. He could not tell him when or if Ewan would recover the full use of his legs. Later at home, hearing the news, Evina, their mother, put her fingertips to her lips. Duncan put a comforting hand on her shoulder then rushed down the grand staircase and strode across the foyer to his office, pacing. He slammed a fist against the wall, moments later pouring himself a whiskey. He gulped it down, blaming Clarissa's rashness for these ill events. Her recent and continuous foolhardy actions tested him.

~ * ~

For a month, Clarissa dove into work, not having discovered anything new she could use to convict Mr. Amberley.

In the shop one evening, Gilbert turned to Clarissa. "I must run an errand. Close up in a little while?"

"Yes. I can manage alone."

"All right, sister. I'll see you soon. Come to our rooms for tea when I return. Harriet wishes for your company."

Not long after he left, a carriage with the Amberley crest arrived. Clarissa inhaled sharply. To her shock and displeasure, Ewan stepped out. She braced herself behind the main counter. He charged in, bringing the scent of moist air with him.

"What are you doing here?" Clarissa stepped back. "How..." She glanced at his legs.

He smirked. "You and I must have words."

"Leave!"

"You have infuriated me and are playing a dangerous game with me."

"I'm not afraid of you," she lied.

"Oh?" He raised his brow. "You should be. You'd better give up this game of yours, and you must convince your family to do the same."

"I have no such intention." Her voice came out coolly; although her heart raced.

He tore around the counter. "You will regret it, but then again... You may not be around long enough to regret it. Unless we could work out a more...suitable agreement between us, continue where we left off."

"I love Duncan."

He studied her with green eyes that matched Duncan's in color, but not in their reflection of honor. "Hmm. Personal threats don't seem to work. You might force me to do something different. If you don't stop your investigation, well, there's always your brother. He could disappear. Or Duncan could suffer an accident that would permanently cripple him—"

"No."

"Whichever situation presents itself to me...one way or the other, I intend to be the victor."

She trembled. "No, you won't be."

He tore off her bonnet and grasped her hair, making her yelp, and forced his mouth over hers, muffling her yells. He cupped a breast. She screamed, and he muted the sound again with another kiss. Finally, he leaned away with a smirk. She lifted her hand to slap him, but he gripped her wrist six inches from his cheek and tossed it down with force.

"The sensation of you, Clarissa. I have dreamt of nothing else." He drew back further. "I wish you weren't so beautiful. I wish I didn't find you so desirable. It has made life difficult for me, but I will do what I am compelled to do. I may force myself on you and make you or your brother disappear." He shoved her away from him.

She collapsed over her counter. Fifteen minutes later, Gilbert returned. He frowned when his notice came to her. Clarissa fussed around the shop, this time holding her tongue, fearing Mr. Amberley would hurt her brother if Gilbert sought retribution.

~ * ~

Duncan went to her shop the next day after having stewed in frustration for weeks. He needed to tell Clarissa how irresponsible she'd been, searching near the squalid alleys and taverns by the docks for that evidence, how brilliantly reckless she was. He walked in and brushed past Gilbert.

Gilbert stepped back, raising a brow in perturbation. Duncan went directly to the back counter, where he saw her unpacking a box within the circle of dim light thrown by an oil lamp. He took note of her sad face, and this knocked his temper down a notch or two. He cleared his throat. She turned to him as he approached her without a word.

"Hello, Duncan." She continued to work, carefully removing two white porcelain Caughley chocolate pots from the box.

"You have no idea how much of my sister's own personal profit was spent on procuring the second chocolate pot for your mother," Gilbert said. "You mentioned she wanted one, and Clarissa wished to buy it herself. It's a Caughley, created in the seventeen-seventies."

"I remember mentioning it," Duncan grumbled.

"With the printed Stalked Apple design. Wonderful blue artistry," Gilbert said.

She smiled. "I've waited a long time for this pot."

Duncan looked at her. "Clarissa, I've a dashed good mind to reprimand you for so much, but you don't appear well." He put gentle fingers against her cheek.

She nuzzled him. "Duncan..." she whispered. "Why have you come here?"

He nudged her chin up. "What aren't you telling me?"

"I...he...uh, I mean, Duncan, you have to leave."

"Pardon me? And if I came here to reconcile with you?" He tested her.

She stiffened.

"Unfortunately, I have a different reason for being here. Who understands *really* why Ewan invited such a beating by saying you were lovers, maybe to give me reason to consider divorcing you? Maybe for revenge, to anger me over ladies in the past for whom we competed, but Clarissa, I found the sleeping tablet. My dog did, actually."

"Oh no! How is he?"

"Unhurt. I've been so angry with you for numerous reasons, the last being the foolishness, which ultimately led to Ewan being confined to bed for so long, possibly permanently but..."

"Duncan, I'm afraid."

"Stop that! He cannot leave the house."

"I don't mean to hurt you. There's something..."

Gilbert was watching avidly, so she lowered her voice. "I found... he..." She flushed.

"What, Clarissa?"

"I can't say."

He leaned closer. "Why? I'm your husband."

"Because I love you. I'm alone in this."

"Tell me what you're hiding."

"I can't."

"I don't like this. I believed there was a chance for us, but you cannot even trust your own husband."

"There is a chance for us, Duncan, only trust me."

"You make that almost impossible, my love."

"If your brother's not arrested...I'm afraid for my life."

Duncan stared at her. Without uttering a further word, he stood, turned on his heel and advanced toward the shop door.

"Don't go."

He stopped. "I cannot abide this situation another moment. Perhaps it was a mistake for me to ask you to marry me."

Crash!

He turned. White pieces of a chocolate pot rested scattered at her feet. Gilbert rushed to her side. Duncan burned with concern but did not speak. He slipped his gloves on and went outside to his coach.

~ * ~

That day, a package arrived for Duncan. He opened it to find a chocolate pot—the surviving of the two. A note read: "Give this to your mother, and give her my love. Most truly yours, Clarissa Hale." Hale—*your maiden name.*

Amberley was crossed out and smudged with water—tears? Hale. *No, your name is Amberley! How I love you, my darling, no matter how we fight. I do not regret marrying you.*

He paced the floor of his office. "She's hiding something she was bursting to tell me."

The next day, he returned to Clarissa's shop. It was empty of patrons for the moment.

Gilbert greeted him with a cautious look. Clarissa was not in attendance.

"Come to make her cry? She's a sensitive soul."

"What, make her cry? No! I merely need to obtain information from her. I regret what I said last I saw her."

Gilbert shrugged. "Well, you missed her. Our little detective has gone on a journey and brought a lady friend to accompany her. I wanted to go, but she was inspired and begged me to let her do it."

"Where did she go?" He took a step closer.

"To the asylum where my wife was supposedly confined." His smirk matched the sarcasm in his voice.

"Why?"

"Detective work."

"Why won't she give this up? My investigator presented me with papers he discovered from one of Napoleon's men, and I showed them to Clarissa. The papers were addressed to—"

"To whom?" Gilbert asked.

"Do you really want this knowledge?"

"Yes."

"Even if it involves your wife?"

"Especially if it involves my wife."

Duncan began carefully. "I'm regretful to say your wife was a spy for Napoleon."

Gilbert inhaled sharply. "Do not slander my wife, Duncan!" He slammed his walking stick to the floor, rattling the floorboards. "What do you want? Revenge for what Clarissa's trying to do to Ewan? Ewan is as guilty as the devil, you fool! And I would kindly ask you never to repeat your words again to anyone unless you want to see my wife hanged!"

"I won't denounce her. I swear it." He tugged on the cuff of his greatcoat. "But that explains where she was previous to being institutionalized."

"She was never in that asylum, Duncan, and Clarissa and I are going to prove it. I would wager your brother planted that evidence, made it fall to your investigator."

He considered Gilbert with sympathy. "You're my brother-in-law, my friend. I detest the situation."

Gilbert gripped the silver top of his walking stick. "So do I. The day we first made your acquaintance, I had a good sense about you. That's why I mentioned our shop. I knew you had no excuse for approaching us in the future. Clarissa was entranced as soon as she saw you."

"I saw her, Gilbert, and my life changed."

"She said the same of you."

Duncan smiled.

"You should be together."

"I'm not sure that's possible. She keeps secrets from me," Duncan said.

Gilbert gestured, pleading with him to understand. "She's desperate not to hurt you, but you cling to the notion that your brother isn't a criminal. Clarissa believes she has no choice but to find evidence to expose him to prevent him harming her or others, and I agree with her."

"You're being ridiculous." Duncan glanced at the large window being dusted with snow then back at Gilbert. "Even if Ewan were a villain, he is presently on the couch, unable to move."

Gilbert rolled his eyes. "I was born lame, and I cope. In fact, growing up, I often surpassed Clarissa at physical games."

"You can walk."

"And he cannot?"

"No!" He paced in front of the counter, agitated.

"Hmm. Well at any rate, I believe you're a good man with a sense of justice and integrity. I hope you get what you want."

Duncan stopped. "But it's the opposite of what Clarissa wants."

"No, it isn't." Gilbert fidgeted with a pile of books on the counter.

Baffled, Duncan took his leave, muttering, "Good day," on the way out.

"Maybe I should do my own personal detective work," he mumbled as he walked away. His stomach turned as he remembered Gilbert's words. *What if Ewan did plant that evidence?*

After some consideration, Duncan came up with a ridiculously dangerous and foolish idea that could ruin him if he were caught. Still, if his wife could risk such danger, then so could he. And it wasn't as if he hadn't faced far worse on the seas.

"*Comment-allez vous? Ou est le vin?* Good. I'm still in practice. I never thought I would go to the little terror himself without trying to kill him. But Bonaparte never saw my face. This might work with a little ingenuity."

Seventeen

Duncan packed his bags then made a call on Ewan, who was reclining on a Grecian couch in his rooms. "I'm going away to take stock of things. You're in charge of the estate during my absence," Duncan announced. "You have a household of servants at your disposal, but do not abuse them."

"Duncan—" Ewan pushed himself to a seated position.

"Goodbye." Duncan strode out of the room and had a footman send for the coach.

When it came around, he went outside. He directed his driver to take him to Clarissa's shop and climbed into the vehicle. Darkness shrouded the city, and snow sparkled under the light cast by lamps as the carriage rattled ahead. At the Hale Emporium, Duncan stepped onto the road. He strode in and greeted Gilbert, standing behind the main counter with a pile of books on each side of him.

"Is she here?"

"Good evening to you, too."

Duncan nodded.

"If you mean Clarissa, she's in her rooms." He glanced over his shoulder.

Duncan swept by him even as Gilbert gestured him past the velvet curtain, which divided the shop from the steps leading to their rooms upstairs. Duncan climbed the creaky stairs and slipped off his gloves, putting them in his coat pockets. At her door, he hesitated, and then knocked. Seconds later, the door creaked open.

"Gil—oh, Duncan. Come in."

She wore a pale spearmint gown with an emerald shawl draped over her shoulders, a stunning effect against her blue-green eyes. He stared, indulging his desire with an erotic fantasy.

"Do you want to come in?"

"Yes." He followed her in.

She closed the door with a click. The strong scent of coffee pervaded his senses. He glanced at her coffee pot on a small dark table.

"Would you care for coffee?"

"No. Thank you. Clarissa, I'm remorseful over my previous, unfortunate words. I did not mean them. You are important to me. Will you forgive me?"

Her features softened, and a smile brightened her face. "Yes."

"I apologize, for so much."

"Me too." She bent and wiped the table around the coffee pot with a folded towel.

"You love me."

Her back stiffened. "Of course, Duncan, I—"

"Tell me what you're hiding."

Her jaw tightened.

His hand went to her shoulder. "Please."

"Yes, but give me time. Will you not give me that as a compromise? Trust my judgment to withhold this for now."

"You'll tell me?"

"Yes."

"All right, but if you do not enlighten me soon, I will ask you again."

"That is fair."

Regarding her, he spoke with soft words, "I miss you. I love you."

"I love you too. Excuse me a moment." She walked by her writing desk and took up a stack of papers, disappearing into her bedroom.

He went in after her, curious, his feet creaking over the wooden floorboards. Seeing her airy room with its yellows and lime green gave him the distinct impression he had walked into a woman's domain. Flower patterns adorned the pale lemon curtains. A watercolor of spring blooms done by her sister-in-law, he knew, hung near her mahogany dressing mirror. An open book laid on a small bookcase on a stand, the pages of one side resting against the metal grill of the front. Next to it sat her walnut writing box with its brass corners and supports she had retrieved from his home. He remembered the day he bought it for her, and how she had thanked him.

She hid her hands behind her back.

"What are those?"

"Letters."

He stepped up to her, close, looking at her from beneath lowered lids. "What do they say?" He used his best husky voice.

Her cheeks flushed pink.

"Give them to me." He reached around her to snatch the papers.

"Duncan, no!"

They fell back onto the bed, he on top of her. The papers landed on the mattress, above her.

He traced her jaw with his fingers. "Do you remember the last time we found ourselves in this position?"

She wiggled beneath him, sighing. It drew an instant response in his trousers.

He kissed her. "Recall what we are together."

"Yes, the exquisite pleasure."

He brushed his lips over her forehead, the tip of her nose, and her lips. His mouth covered hers, his tongue probing, demanding, but at the same time, he hoped. He drew away, awaiting her permission.

"Duncan," she whispered, and put her palms to his chest but did not push him away.

"You are my wife."

"I am. You are delighted with that."

"Immensely." He planted a kiss on her bosom, and her back arched.

"I missed you."

"And I you." He glided his fingers down her side, grasping the silken material of her gown. "Will we be interrupted?" he asked between kisses.

"No. If we're in here for a time, Gilbert will rejoice for us and not knock on my door for the world."

"I see. I hope we come to an understanding. You entrance me. And," he said, "I want to thank you for the gift to my mother. It meant a lot to me, as it did to her. I should buy you the company."

She sighed again, but this time it sounded sad, even as she kissed him. "I want us to be together."

Article by article, they peeled off each other's clothes. He smoothed his fingertips down her waist and ended at her thigh over her goose-pimpled skin.

He stopped. "You are beautiful, and it goes deeper than merely your face and body. I pray our families don't tear us apart."

They lay down. She leaned up to brush her lips with his. "Is this right?"

He blinked in surprise. "Yes. I haven't touched another woman."

"Would you ever?"

"Would you go to another man?"

"I would rather die."

"You mean that." He paused, overcome.

"Duncan?"

"I will never betray you. I haven't betrayed you. And I will never look into another woman's eyes. The disappointment would send me to the depths of despair if you and I were not reconciled."

She jerked him into an urgent kiss. He covered her breasts with loving kisses and lifted her arms.

He traced her bottom lip with the pad of his thumb. "I searched the globe for you, on my ship."

She fluttered long lashes, and his heart skipped a beat.

"My sense of yearning went on for years. Nothing quelled the empty ache inside. Then you walked into my life, at my own home! I felt joy. I felt complete." He caressed a light brown curl and dusted the soft lock aside.

She moved, and something crinkled. He looked up and saw a piece of paper next to her hair. She shifted and reached for her notes, but he was faster. He grasped the paper and read it, mumbling the words aloud.

Sharp disappointment cut through him. He sat up. "This is singularly depressing."

She pushed into a seated position. "I regret you weren't aware a doctor at Colney Hatch Asylum is a long-time friend of your brother's."

"The papers must be a hoax. Why do you pursue this? Don't you care about me? My family?"

"W...what? Do you really believe I don't?"

"Not with this behavior."

She trembled. Her shoulders slumped as if in defeat. "Unbelievable."

"What is?"

"Your foolishness." She was silent a moment. "Why are you so dim-witted?"

Duncan slammed a fist onto the mattress. "There are things of which you are not aware." He slipped back into his clothing.

She put on her chemise, deciding against the stays, then her drawers, petticoat, and green dress.

"Someone in my family died because of me, and I won't make a mistake like that again." He straightened his cravat.

"What? That would explain why you're so protective of your brother. Tell me what happened."

"I'm leaving."

"Do not go home." She grabbed his arm.

"Have you lost your senses?" He tore his arm from her grasp.

"Please!"

"Why are you so troubled?"

Her raw fright gave him shudders.

"Because your brother—"

"Ewan what?"

"He—"

He glanced at the bed then back at her. "I wasn't going home. I'm leaving to go abroad."

"Abroad? Good!"

"You want me gone?"

She brought pleading eyes to him. "I merely want you away from him."

"Why?"

"Something happened. He—"

He studied her.

"Take me with you." Her lip quivered.

He curled his fingers around her arm. "No. It would be risky."

"Where are we going?"

"Clarissa—"

"My love...*Please.*"

"It's dangerous."

"Such a thing does not vex me, as long as I'm by your side. If you left me here, though, it's a certainty you'd come back a widower." Her beseeching gaze tore at his resistance.

He embraced her trembling form, rubbing her back in comfort. "You're terrified. All right. I'll take you. It's fortunate you speak French, or you would have to pretend being mute. And French manners and customs?"

She withdrew from him. "Of course, but what does that have to do with anything?"

"We are to be *Monsieur et Madame*—what French name do you fancy?"

"Where are we going?"

"To see Emperor Napoleon Bonaparte."

She paled and fell backward. He caught her around the waist inches from the mattress.

~ * ~

They watched from the deck while they crossed the rough waters of the English Channel. Duncan wrapped his arms around Clarissa, who was almost doubled over, her complexion tinged green.

"This will pass. You will grow accustomed to the journey."

"I hope so." She focused past the sails and not at the churning water below.

"Winter is the worst time of year to travel."

"Duncan, are we actually going to...enter Napoleon's camp?"

"We will be following them. Spying sometimes requires such things."

"Sp...spying."

"Remember, as *reporters* documenting—"

"Napoleon. Is this really for the Prince of Wales, our regent?" She put her palm to the railing.

"Not as our main goal, but if we discover anything interesting, I will report it. My previous work has given me useful political privileges."

"You enjoyed influence in the Navy," she muttered.

He smiled in response. "We are here to either clear up your sister-in-law's name, and I would beg your forgiveness and admit to my stupidity, or prove her guilty, in which case—"

"In which case?" Clarissa shifted her weight from foot to foot.

"I'm not sure, but I'm afraid it would seriously hurt our marriage." She gasped.

"You have to understand, Clarissa, I wouldn't report her, but for a man of my convictions and political loyalties, well, you would be forcing me to go against my deepest values."

"You would spare her, save her from being prosecuted, for me? Even though I—"

"Yes." He glanced at the choppy water. "But I would have to look into your face and remember you encouraged me to betray England."

She crinkled his coat sleeve between her fingers. "You make me sound like a traitor. I would die for England, Duncan. I love my country."

He regarded her. "I am aware of this. We are stuck in an impossible situation. Your motivations are built on love for your sister, but I can't be happy for it."

"Your reasons are built on love for your brother, but I don't approve of you standing by and defending a criminal." A tear slid down her cheek.

He gently wiped it away. "Don't cry. Things will be understood once and for all. Sweetheart, I believe you and Ewan were never lovers."

"Even if I were a woman of loose morals, which I am not, Ewan does not suit me, being far from the man you are."

"I still despise what you did. It was dangerous and stupid, but it told me you aren't afraid of a little risk. But still...You should not have seen such an intimate scar."

"I'm sorry."

"Your sister-in-law might have been his lover and feared retribution. If she could spy for France, then she's clever enough to think up this scenario."

Clarissa took a steadying breath. "Her spying is impossible. She and I have been friends since we were girls of eight."

"Then why do you look so disturbed?" He caressed her cheek with the back of his fingers.

"It's the seasickness."

"Ah, I see. Mrs. Hale's being a former spy and Ewan's former lover is no madder than the idea of my brother killing a girl."

"By accident, to be fair, and even you admitted he was troubled."

"Yes, he's forever been difficult, but that does not make him a villain, and I have to protect our mother."

"So, if you had proof Harriet's accusations were accurate?"

"If that unlikely situation came to pass—"

She fidgeted with the ribbons of her bonnet. He tied it for her.

"Would you denounce him to the authorities?" she asked.

He stared at her.

"Well?"

He rubbed his brow with his fingertips. "The idea makes me ill."

"What would you do? Hypothetically?"

"If you weren't my wife, I would have dismissed you moments ago. I'd turn him in and hope for the best. As far as that street girl is concerned, it's tragic, but an accident is an accident."

"Abduction and violating a woman are not accidents." She pushed a fist against her thigh.

He shook his head in disbelief. "There's no possibility he could have behaved in that way, and we are going to prove it."

"Harriet is going to be proven innocent, and you and I will live our lives in bliss. I will fill your days with devotion. And I won't rub your stupidity in." Her lips formed a teasing grin.

"God, let her be innocent."

"What?" Clarissa chuckled.

"But wait, no. That, along with Ewan's friendship with Dr. Dearborn—if it's true—would point to Ewan probably being guilty." He wrapped his fingers around hers.

"Is your brother good to your family?"

"No. He continually caused my parents anguish with one scheme after another."

"Then why, Duncan?"

"He's my brother, my *last* one."

"You would let him ruin your good family name? He will eventually."

"I have been able to clean up his messes." He released her.

"It's not your duty to do so!"

He glanced down. "It is. I am the eldest now." He encircled her waist with his arm. "I love you so much, and I'm deuced sorry for this trouble."

~ * ~

That night, a cabin boy with tousled blond hair and soiled clothes approached them while they dined.

"Do not be afraid," Duncan said. "Have you something to tell us?"

He bowed. "Sir, where do I start?"

"At the beginning."

"My uncle is aboard. He wishes to discuss something with you."

Duncan's brow rose.

"I will meet with you later tonight concerning the details." The boy bowed and turned on his heel to leave.

Continuing their dinner, Duncan and Clarissa discussed politics. He knew she kept well informed with her books and newspapers, and reveled in the fact that he had chosen such a rare woman with whom to share such conversations.

"You are aware of Napoleon's policies with Russia?" he asked.

"He would put them in a severe economic crisis over Britain. Tsar Alexander won't have it."

"I'm gratified to hear you're informed."

She blushed.

"Ah, Clarissa Amberley."

"Duncan."

"I am also gratified you like my name. It belonged to my maternal grandfather, a Scottish Highlander."

She expelled a small sigh. "I adore Scotland."

"So do I."

"I want you to take me to the Highlands. I want to wear your clan tartan and dance to Scottish music."

"I want to unwrap my clan tartan from your body and—"

"And what?"

"You would be beautiful in a Highland lass's attire, guiding sheep along those rolling hills at the height of summer."

"Surrounded by the divine heather. I would drop my shepherdess's stick as soon as I saw my romantic Highland warrior approach me with longing."

"Your hair would tumble over your bosom."

She cleared her throat. "The Russian issue."

You're still offended from the last time we touched, and I displayed such disappointment in you.

He clasped his hands on the splintered table and inhaled deeply of air thick with the smell of the sea. "Russia bases its economy on exporting raw goods to Britain in exchange for manufactured goods. They require this exchange in order to prevent economic collapse."

"Why is he trying to destroy Russia economically, Duncan? Have you heard anything?"

"It's not his intention. But he is outraged at what he sees as insubordination. A few years ago, in 1807, he rendezvoused with the tsar who told him he hated the English as much as he did, and Napoleon considered it an act of peace between them. He now feels betrayed."

"So, Tsar Alexander became his ally and agreed to refuse commercial trade with Britain at all, hence the continental blockade."

Impressed with her insightfulness, he warmed with pride. "Napoleon believed the alliance between their two empires would bring peace and calm Europe. He went to Portugal who wouldn't abide the blockade. Spain became involved. Napoleon made his brother the king of Spain and put soldiers there. He mistakenly thought the Spanish would welcome joining his empire."

"I assume they didn't."

"No, and the war was going badly there, brutal and bloody."

"Mark my words, he will fall. His Spanish war was not for glory."

"His judgment is becoming impaired."

"If he goes to war with Russia..." She shifted on her narrow bench. The ship swayed, and she grimaced.

"My dear, are you well?"

"Yes."

He gave a thoughtful glance up at the splintering boards above their heads. "The emperor is assembling a large army to go up against Russia. A number are French, but thousands are not."

"All this to punish the tsar. Could he win?"

"Possibly, but if you ask me, he won't. He has become...well, a fool, relying only on his own will and not the better judgment of others." He took a sip of ale, glancing at her plate.

She wasn't eating her food.

"Our General Wellington arrived to help. He got combined forces with the Spanish and the Portuguese. They recently beat the French, is that so, Duncan?"

"Yes, in January. At Ciudad Rodrigo."

"I imagine French morale is sinking. Austria became inspired."

"Yes. They saw what happened in Spain. They had taken Napoleon's abuse themselves. They wanted to inspire a large scale revolution against him, hoping to liberate several neighboring countries."

"Unfortunately, Bavaria rallied around Napoleon. He once again beat the Austrians. Later they signed a peace treaty, but Francis the First had to give Napoleon three million of his subjects," she said.

"You do read a lot."

"I do when I'm not working. Anyway, negotiations with Russia have failed."

He rubbed his cheeks, tired. "The Russian army concentrated its forces on its borders. Napoleon is filling out his own ranks from around the empire. You might need to speak Polish or Italian or German to communicate with his soldiers now."

She poked at the bland cod on her plate with her fork. "He hopes to overwhelm the Russians with his numbers."

"Numbers aren't as important as strategy."

"And good judgment."

"I agree," he said. "Napoleon hoped to influence the tsar again first, but an ally of mine said he was heard to say that if he didn't, then Russia was doomed. It would be crushed under his hatred of England."

"What if Napoleon's foreign recruits do not want to die for him?" she asked.

"I'm sure they do not."

"Napoleon almost invaded Britain in 1805."

"At that time, he had two thousand ships and two hundred thousand soldiers. But at the end of the summer, he ordered them to turn back and march into Europe."

"I think about the battle of Trafalgar."

Duncan stiffened.

"What is it?"

"Mention of that battle."

"What happened? I mean you must have inside information, things of which the public wasn't notified."

"I was there."

She gave him a stunned look.

"On a ship?" she asked wide-eyed.

"Those in the Royal Navy generally are. What happened that day, October twenty-first, 1805, it was glorious, and it was horrible. We lost my commander, Admiral Horatio Nelson."

"He was your commander, England's greatest sailor? You were on the flagship, *The Victory*?"

"Yes, and fortunate to be there. I impressed the right people."

"What was that like?"

He gave her a long, thoughtful look. "I could discuss it for hours."

"What are your impressions of him?"

"He was intelligent concerning many issues, big and small."

"I would imagine. Being at sea for extended periods must have taken its toll on you."

"Admiral Nelson believed good health was imperative in the service. He thought it would be much easier for his men to maintain their continued good health than to have to be cured of a medical problem, so he saw that we ate properly."

"I am glad to hear that," she said.

"Also, we received inoculations against certain diseases such as smallpox."

She gave him a tender look. "I want to comprehend more of your life on board a ship, your adolescence and early adulthood."

"Such as?"

She shrugged. "Pick something at random to tell me, a piece in your daily life."

"Let me ponder this...hmm. The officers were not often together at once. Mealtime was one of those few times. We were seated at a long table in the wardroom."

"How did you prepare food on board a ship?"

"On the forward of the ship's galley stove, the kitchen stove. We could grill it, or bake it, or if we wanted to, use a spit. The crew's food was boiled though. I had that until I was an officer."

She plunked her fork down and allowed him to curl his fingers around hers. "And now, tell me of your service in the Navy."

"I risked execution for what I did."

She gasped.

Eighteen

Duncan took a sip of ale and set his mug down as their cabin swayed. Under the flickering light of a lantern, he could make out Clarissa's pale face. "Sweetheart, are you certain you are feeling quite the thing?"

She wasn't taking too well to the sea, and he was concerned. Once they hit land, it would be a hard trip to Russia.

"I am well, thank you. Tell me what happened on your ship."

He tapped his fingers on the cool wood. "If we were traveling alongside in fleet, I would invite the other captains and officers to join me for the evening meal. We reveled in the entertainment of sharing battle stories and more amusing anecdotes as well."

She plucked at the fringe of her moss green shawl. "The Impress Service—"

"To recruit. At the start of a journey, at least a third of our men needed to be already trained, in order to launch our ship off properly. A few were recruited among merchants. Other sailors were gained from the press."

She released the fringe and picked up her spoon, hovering it above her soup bowl. "I should hope none of the terrible stories I've heard were true."

His narrow bench creaked as he bent forward. "What have you heard?"

She put down her spoon, her soup hardly tasted. "There were those who were rendered unconscious, and others were threatened at sword point, pistol and musket, or otherwise coerced to join the crews of ships."

"That is unfortunately true."

"Have you ever witnessed this?" Her blue-green gaze came up to meet his.

"Yes, in my younger years. It made such an impression on me, well later—"

"The American incident."

"Yes. I thought those men no traitors to England. They hailed from a different country. Had they been deserters, I would have acted differently. A 1740 law states that foreigners cannot be pressed into service, but the Navy often circumvented this." He thought of that day.

"How?"

"A man who married an English citizen could become English by naturalization. Also, if a foreigner had served for at least two years on a British merchant ship, he could become pressed, forced into the Navy. America and England disagreed over what made a person a citizen."

She picked up her spoon again but didn't use it. "What did America require for citizenship?"

She was so charming in her quest for erudition. "Among other ways, some who had spent at least two years serving on an American ship could become citizens."

"This group you were going to press—"

He glanced at her bowl and plate. "You're not eating much."

"My appetite has diminished since I boarded this ship."

"Try to eat."

She took a spoonful of soup. "It's bland but adequate. Now I will suffer no more delays. Tell me."

"I saw desperation in their faces. They pleaded with me concerning their devotion to America and their families at home. They discussed

America's beauty. By the way they carried on, I knew they were American and not merely trying to find their way out of service."

"I see. Go on."

"The Americans said the Royal Navy could not have her sailors. Certain of my men believed a man born a British subject was still British. He had no right to renounce that and turn away from his duty. Remember, we needed a strong Navy with which to fight Napoleon. How could a sailor prove he was American and find his way off a British ship? That was difficult. The nation was too young to have created its own true accent. They gave their citizens a paper called a *Protection*."

"Did not those men you rescued have this protection?"

"My admiral was on board at the time, visiting. His ship was nearby. The men were brought to me. My admiral claimed they bought their papers from an American selling them, someone who had gone to several notaries to get them."

"Forgeries."

"Anyone could get the papers from these notaries by saying they were American."

"But you believed the Americans. You let them go?"

"I quietly released them from containment, gave them supplies and a small boat, and told them to move for shore. I never saw them again."

"I'm sure you were greatly reprimanded."

"When my superiors discovered this, yes, but they investigated and attained proof I had been correct about those men. If the sailors had not been American, my superiors might have made an example of me."

Clarissa considered him in the low yellowish glow of the lantern light. Her eyes glistened, speaking of pride for him. She reached across the scarred table for his fingers.

He kissed her knuckles then held on. "I lost my chance for advancement, but my previous service earned me a respectable retirement because I had helped win more than a few battles for England. Besides, I was needed at home. Retirement hasn't been so bad, though. I enjoy running my family estate."

"Do you miss the Navy?"

He straightened. A knock sounded on the cabin door. He rose to open it.

The boy who had spoken to them earlier was there. "It's me, Tom. Come with me to see my uncle."

Duncan reached for Clarissa, and they followed the skinny lad. Clarissa shivered as the biting winter wind stung her, and Duncan put a protective arm around her shoulders. Tom led them to a cabin and knocked. It creaked open.

Long oily strands of gray hair framed an unshaven face, and the man wore a soiled blue uniform. He squinted at them. "I've been expecting you." He retreated to allow Clarissa and Duncan to enter.

A few candles and a dusty lantern shed the only light in air stale with mold. The man gestured to a table and bench, and everyone sat down.

He rested his arms on the table and considered them. "I perceive things of the future."

"Are you a seer?" Clarissa burst out.

The man grinned, showing missing teeth, and rubbed his whisker-rough chin. "My name is Sam, and yes, you could say I have a bit of awareness of what's to come." Sam regarded Duncan. "I see danger ahead."

"In Russia?"

"Yes. More than normal."

"There's going to be *extraordinary* danger in Russia?" Clarissa asked.

"Yes. My visions have shown me an encompassing cloud of grave danger. This year of 1812 will not soon be forgotten, mark my words." Sam smirked. "Also, you must take a care returning to England, for trouble awaits you there."

"What do you want from us?" Duncan asked.

"You don't believe me, but you will. You'll see what happens to Napoleon's men and horses."

Duncan took Clarissa's arm. "My good sir, you—"

"You will see for yourself."

Weary, Duncan rubbed his jaw.

"Napoleon will lead his massive army into misery, following the Russians into their country, a country only the Russians fathom how to survive in winter. The Russians will retreat, burning the land, and Napoleon's men will starve. Disaster, Mr. Amberley, Mrs. Amberley, and you shall also descend into your own darkness."

Duncan dragged a pale Clarissa from the cabin. He didn't believe a word of what Sam had said, but his wife obviously did, for she sobbed. They discussed it once they were in their cabin.

"Darling, he was mad. Pray don't heed a word he said."

"But he seemed so sure."

He cupped her cheek. "You trust me?"

"Yes."

"Trust me to protect you. I will bring you home to England safe and protect you there."

A smile broke out on her face. He gave her a lingering kiss.

~ * ~

The next day, Duncan faced his wife over breakfast. "I am not privy to enough concerning you."

"Gilbert was always my best friend. Then I was introduced to Harriet in 1799. She had a strange accent at that time. I no longer remember exactly what it was. It faded quickly because her parents hired a tutor to teach them how to pronounce English correctly. From the day we met Harriet, the three of us chased each other around the streets of Islington."

"You were close," he presumed.

"Yes. When Harriet, who is my age, came of age, Gilbert courted her. They have been a fairytale couple since."

Duncan smiled. The musty room smelled of eggs. "How long have they been married?"

"Four years."

"She was sixteen?"

"Yes. And Gilbert nineteen. Both our parents and hers were thrilled for the marriage."

"My mother was overjoyed when I married you. I regret the situation we're in at present. I don't want to hurt you. I can't think how I want this to end. If my brother weren't at risk of being executed, it might be different. But—"

"You now suspect—"

"He might be guilty. If your sister-in-law is proven to be a former spy, that could mean Ewan never abducted her, and Dr. Dearborn lied to help him. But then...I don't understand why Mrs. Hale would lie about Ewan. Why would she want him punished?"

Coffee steam rose from her tin cup. "Why did your brother and Dr. Dearborn spin falsehoods about Harriet being institutionalized, even earlier than you received the letter from your investigator from France?"

He shifted on the creaking bench. "I don't know that they did, but if so, it was to show that he was innocent? I mean, he didn't do it, but he had no evidence, so he contrived some, possibly."

"They had met formerly." She reached up and tilted the lantern, making it shed more light onto the cabin's small table.

"Possibly they were lovers, he turned her away, and she did this for revenge."

Her chin came up a notch. "She loves Gilbert. And Harriet is my treasured friend. I love her as much as if she were my own sister. After Papa died, I cried on her shoulder for months. She saw me through the tragedy of his loss. I'm sad you and your brother aren't that close."

A chill black silence surrounded them, but he hid his uneasy sentiments.

"If he were judged guilty of those horrible crimes, I would have to spend years comforting my mother and I would have to shun Ewan."

She didn't say a word.

Nineteen

In May, they arrived near the Russian border and secured lodgings at a Polish inn.

Inside their room, Clarissa faced Duncan near a small wooden table. "I would rather we were in France. I'm afraid."

"Napoleon is here. We will get the information we need and leave as quickly as possible, hopefully without incident."

"Now that we're so close to Russia, maybe I should tell you something."

"Oh?" He looked at her enquiringly.

"Then again maybe not."

"Clarissa, do not trifle with me."

She took a step within the small confines of their room. A flicker of apprehension coursed through her. "What I have to say concerns your brother."

"Go on."

"You've had time away from him to logically see he might be capable of more than you thought."

"Sadly, that is true, but I hold out hope he did not do the worst."

"I am more comfortable discussing this now that we're far away from him. In England, I'm afraid we had a confrontation."

"What sort of confrontation? How?"

"He came to the shop speaking terrible things to me."

"But...he was incapacitated."

"No, he was not."

"Clarissa?"

She went to his side, taking a hold of his arm. Creases of concern formed around his eyes.

"You know I'm telling you the truth. He could and did walk...to see me in the shop."

He curled his fingers around hers with a sharp nod. "Fine. I believe you. He was always prone to exaggerating injuries."

"Thank you."

"What the devil did he say to you?"

"I don't want to hurt you."

"Tell me."

"You won't believe me," she said.

"Please. I will."

Her shoulders fell as she sighed. "Gilbert was off doing an errand, and your brother probably waited until he left, so he could approach me. He threatened to violate me and worse."

"He did...*what*?" His lips formed a tight line, and he squared his shoulders.

She looked away briefly. "You don't believe me."

"I've spent time getting to know your mannerisms, sensing you in a profound way. You're not lying."

"Thank you."

"Tell me he didn't actually—"

"He did not. You know your brother so well. Can you not sense his lies?"

"No. I was never able to, oddly. His face looks the same whether he's lying or not."

"He also—it's hard for me to say."

The warmth of his hand enveloped hers. "Tell me. Even if you... encouraged him by that brash thing you did, it's no excuse for vile behavior on his part."

Her bottom lip trembled. "He hurt me. He grasped me by my hair and forced a kiss on me, promising worse." But she wouldn't say what that was.

"Damn him!" Duncan spun from her and pressed a fist to the dingy wall above their bed.

She waited until he turned to her, his eyes cold.

"The moment we arrive home, I will inform him he is to leave my house at once. I'll not tell him why at first, so as not to scare him into running, and give him money, for our mother's sake, but just enough to keep him near until you and I can conclude once and for all if he is guilty or not of the criminal charges against him. And if the bastard ever comes near you again, I'll do more than banish him."

She threw herself into his arms, grateful to finally have her husband back. He held her close.

~ * ~

Clarissa and Duncan sat in their room at the inn for weeks in Poland, pretending to be French writers chronicling Napoleon. She was glad to have learned from a tutor borrowed from her well-to-do relative, and practiced for endless hours to strengthen her French language skills.

One morning she and Duncan sat with a large pot of hot coffee between them on the table in their room. Duncan looked up from reading a copy of the local Polish newspaper dated the previous June, tapping it against the table.

He had paid a local fluent in French to translate for him. "Tensions are high because Napoleon is assembling his Grand Armeé."

"West of the Russian border?"

"Yes."

She wrapped her fingers around a cup of steaming black coffee. As its vapors rose to warm her face, she inhaled its aroma and sipped. Bitterness coated her tongue. Not used to such an inferior brand, she crinkled her nose. Then she reminded herself she was lucky to have any at all since it was so hard to come by then.

"Are you ready for this task, to discover the truth about your sister-in-law?"

She gulped. "Yes."

"Sweetheart, do you want to do this? Following the army will be risky."

"I'm no coward. Let's do what we came to do and go home and begin our lives again *together*."

He reached for and gave her fingers a squeeze.

"What are you thinking?"

"That you're an uncommonly brave woman."

"And my daring does not...offend you?"

He rubbed her knuckles with his thumb. "Your rash behavior in the past has caused me much grief, but your courage fills me with pride and thrilling anticipation."

"Thank you. You're coming to accept my strangeness."

"I always did. From the start. Let's check our supplies."

With both arms, he picked up a bag of flour he'd been meaning to move out of the way and heaved it onto the bed. Across its canvas surface, it read: *sand.*

"That will deceive some. It should suffice for weeks, providing bland biscuits and bread."

She patted a box of radishes. "Mm, delicious." She chuckled and glanced at a barrel of wine near the box.

He deposited a basket of eggs beside it. "The generous farmer charged me twice what I'd normally pay. He made me pay four times the going rate for the horse and carriage, but I had anticipated that and brought an ample amount."

"And rice." She swung to her right.

"Oats and fruit."

"Not fine cuisine, but it will keep us alive."

"Yes."

"Wait here. I will return presently with information on anything that might lead to insights on your sister-in-law's mystery." He kissed her and left their cramped room.

~ * ~

An hour had passed when Duncan strode through the door. Clarissa put her book down as he sank beside her on the bed.

"The emperor is furious. His supposed ally, Russia, refused to take part any longer in his blockade of Britain's goods."

Clarissa considered him, moved as usual by his emerald eyes. She remembered him in the blue naval attire he had worn the day they encountered each other for the first time. Now here he was in his rough attire as a spy. Course brown linen hung from his muscular frame. He wore his trousers well over brown boots spotted with shiny marks of age.

"What have you ascertained from the man I assume you paid well?"

"Over drinks we discoursed on the glory of France and Napoleon. I told him what he wanted to hear. He told me he would be happy to fill the pages of my Paris gazette with Napoleon's glorious and brave activities. We agreed to meet again."

"I'm proud of you."

"Thank you." His lips stretched into a smile.

"What position does this man hold?"

"He's part of the imperial guard."

She gasped. "Napoleon's...Imperial...Guard? Duncan, they are directly under the emperor's control. Veteran soldiers, the most feared in his army."

"There are sixty thousand of them here."

"Personal bodyguards," she continued, in awe. "Not committed to battle except as a last resort."

"Yes." He grinned.

"What was he like, Duncan, this bodyguard?"

"Tall, strongly built."

"As I would expect."

"He has an intent look, which is a bit hostile, from what I've seen while he was working, but I caught him when he was relaxed, away from Napoleon, off-duty, and we drank, he far more than me."

"Why him?"

"I saw my opening. My experience in the Navy made me a good judge of men, so I applied it."

"Be careful."

He smiled. "Careful, I perceived a hint of a British accent. We must stick to the French and stay in practice."

"Oh." She touched her lips. "Would you like wine?"

"Thank you. I'll have a glass."

She rose to pour glasses of wine.

He took a sip. "I almost forgot what I started to say. Napoleon went to the Russian ambassador last year to inquire about the troops at the border. He left angry. His advisors told him not to invade Russia, but here we are. He believes he won't be here long. I disagree. As soon as we procure the information we need, we are leaving in a hurry. If you hear this term: *Les Pekins*, the Muftis, in reference to us, it means civilians."

"Oh."

"You may learn a bit of army slang since we're camped relatively close. I must become friendly with them. It's good that I made friends with a man in the Imperial Guard. His closeness to *Le Patron*, the boss, could be useful in discovering the names of spies."

She stared at him, giving him her keen attention as he continued.

~ * ~

Clarissa sat in the tavern near the Russian border, waiting for Duncan to return. He had only left on a short errand to speak with someone. The barman tried to speak to her, and she twisted her handkerchief.

"Bah! The French!" he spat, and then left her to herself.

A French capitaine approached her. His black hair gleamed in the lights of lanterns hanging on hooks around the walls. He was a smug presence, standing there. The smile in his eyes contained a telltale blue flame.

"Madame."

An unwelcome surge of excitement coursed through her, and she denied what it really was. The fine-looking man made her tremble with terror.

"*Oui, c'est Madame Ollivier*. My husband is to join me presently." She averted her eyes.

"The newspaper man. I suppose your stories are going well?"

"Yes."

"I would be happy to answer any questions you may have. After all, our citizens should hear of the glory of our Emperor."

"Of course. Thank you."

He lifted her chin and gasped. "My pardon, Madame."

Her glance landed on the sword hanging at his side. "Your knife, is it uncomfortable to wear?" she mocked.

He laughed. "Knife? My dear lady, this is a saber. It has ended the lives of more than a few British soldiers."

She trembled.

"I'm regretful to offend your female sensibilities. I assumed, since you are here, that you've seen blood."

"Yes, of course I have. It doesn't mean I like it."

"No, of course not."

She looked past him, and her heart jumped with happiness the minute Duncan entered the room. She stood and extended her arms. "Henri!"

Duncan kissed her hand. "Darling." Facing the *capitaine*, he scrutinized him. "Have you any concern with my wife?"

"I was merely offering to answer any questions Madame might have."

"Would you be willing to answer mine?" Duncan's tone dripped with caution.

"Of course. France's glory must be documented."

"Yes, it must," Duncan said. "What does the emperor intend?"

"He wants to launch the war and crush the Russians in quick combat. Afterwards, we will then march to Moscow. The tsar will negotiate for peace, and then we'll return to France. Napoleon will be the undisputed ruler in Europe."

"When—" Duncan started.

"We invade tomorrow." Warning colored the *capitaine's* voice. "I advise you to take the utmost care. Stay away from the battle. You can visit the battlefield afterward and question the men." He clasped his hands in his lap. "And Monsieur, keep that pretty wife with you from now on. Napoleon can attest to the honor of the French, but we have over six hundred thousand soldiers, and not even two hundred thousand of them are French."

Is he mad, to make such a blanket statement regarding their honor? Clarissa thought.

"*Je comprends.*"

The *capitaine* nodded to Duncan, gave a gentlemanly bow to Clarissa, and strode out of the room.

~ * ~

"June twenty-fourth, 1812. Napoleon invades Russia, crossing the Nieman River," Duncan said, absently, but matter-of-factly, staring ahead. He tossed Clarissa a glance. "Sound like a good headline?"

"Indeed."

They sat in their big-wheeled wagon pulled by a single horse. From a safe distance, he and Clarissa looked ahead at the line of men.

"This defies the senses." Her tone sparkled with wonder. "There are Italians—"

"And Poles," he said.

"French and Germans..." She gestured with open palms, pointing toward the army ahead.

"Napoleon hopes the sheer numbers of his army will be enough to attain his goal."

She clucked her tongue. "We're going deep into enemy territory."

After glancing at her, he watched the men again. "The Russians are on the retreat."

"Duncan, I mean, Henri, there will be deserters." She patted his arm.

"Yes. It's the biggest army I've ever seen, massive, and swarming across the frontier."

"This is the adventure of my life. I could die at any moment."

He curled his fingers around hers. "I will protect you with my life."

She rested her cheek against his chest. He skimmed the length of her back, and she shivered. A scan around told him much. Men filled the field in front of them. Horses, servants and camp followers milled about, while soldiers fidgeted, tense as if in preparation. The officers seemed to have a carriage, and the generals appeared to be in possession of more than a solitary vehicle.

Clarissa raised her face to Duncan, his attention fixed on the artillery parks and pontoon bridges. "Some are so young."

"A couple of young fellows said they have never seen a war."

"Why are they here?"

"To make their fortunes," he stated matter-of-factly.

"Where are the Russians?"

"Napoleon must be asking himself the same thing."

A loud crack shook the air. Clarissa grasped his arm.

He put his arms around her. "Thunder. Look. Clouds are rolling in faster than horses racing on a track."

Lightning danced across the sky. Hailstones crashed, and raindrops plopped onto them.

He led her underneath the wagon's cover, lowering the canvas flap and securing it with a rope. "Good Navy canvas. Even in the harshest storm, it did well for my crew onboard ship, so that's why I brought it to protect our carriage."

She rested her head on his lap. Gentle fingers caressed stray locks. They spoke a few moments longer, and before slipping under their blanket to sleep that night, they scrubbed their skin clean with wet rags—dampened from the water of a river. She hoped in the future, they could find the water from the wells of towns, with a bit of soap added—and that they would be able to do this regularly.

~ * ~

Days dragged by. As the army traveled, the men came across peasants' villages, but no enemy soldiers. Creaking along in their cumbersome wagon behind the army, Duncan observed the poor state of the peasants, the sad state of their dress, coarse trousers, and simple shirts. He groaned as they passed ransacked villages, barns and grain fields stripped bare. Wherever Napoleon's troops had passed, the towns were ravaged, the innocent citizens ruined.

Two weeks passed, and the Russians still wouldn't fight. They were up against a much larger army and preferred to retreat.

One night from their camp behind the army, Duncan surveyed Clarissa across the firelight. He raised his chin to the expanse of the black sky in which a billion stars twinkled then looked at his beautiful wife chewing a biscuit, and motioned her close. She put the morsel down and came to him.

"Duncan...I'm afraid. I've never seen blood coming from gaping sword wounds and don't wish to. I don't want to see soldiers run through with sabers. You know we overheard them say that food is getting harder to come by. The countryside...war is ruining it. I saw several hayfields wantonly flattened. It could become dangerous for us."

"That's why I keep most of our supplies out of sight, tied underneath our carriage. It's also why I leave you holding a pistol and forage with the horse—looking for something for it to eat, supposedly in search of food for us—to appear to the soldiers that we are no better off than they are, but our supplies should last well beyond the time we'll be here."

He added, "Thousands of men have disappeared, predicting disaster, starving, and raiding houses along the countryside. If we are approached, appear hungry, as if you haven't eaten in two days. I have packed a few items of clothing that are a little big."

"So did I, as you advised me to. My gowns are becoming as battered and soiled as your attire despite my efforts to care for them and scrub them whenever we come across a source of water."

"We might need to wear the big clothes. It will make us appear hungrier and protect us from raids."

"I hear soldiers are discouraged by horses stretched out dead along the road." She shuddered. "It makes me sad to see the horses, Duncan."

"I as well, my love." He considered the distant military encampment.

She saw tents lined up and a long string of campfires flickering under the moonlight. A strange twittering sounded behind her.

She jumped and grasped his shirt. He hissed.

"What was that?"

He peeled her fingers away. "Sweetheart, I need to breathe."

"Oh, sorry." She let go.

He took a deep breath. "It was a bird."

"A bird?"

"Yes." He motioned her to return to his side. "Let me hold you."

"I would like that very much. Take my mind off this place."

He wrapped his arms around her. "Would you hear something funny?"

"Yes."

"Napoleon said the English Channel is a mere ditch and that England is a nation of shopkeepers."

She grinned.

"Let's discuss your family."

"My brother is so happy with Harriet. When they arrived in England, she and her family immersed themselves in English culture and tried to erase signs of what they were."

"Why did they do so?"

"To begin again. Her father procured work as a merchant in England."

"What was her accent?"

"I'm not sure. I think maybe Germanic. Her parents forbade her to discuss from where they came, but I overheard her say the name Maximilian."

"The Fourth?"

"I think so."

"He ascended the throne of Bavaria in 1799."

"That was the year Harriet's family moved to England, the year I made her acquaintance. It's feasible they weren't fond of their new leader. Bavaria, hmm, a German kingdom."

"The French Republic took territory from them."

A shot exploded yards behind them. Shouts pierced the air. Hooves pounded.

Duncan helped her up. He raced with her to their wagon, swiping up the sword from inside.

"Get underneath!" he ordered.

She slid under it, and he joined her, their stomachs against cold earth.

He put his arm around her shoulders. "Shh."

She trembled, and he hugged her.

"*Merde*!" A French soldier stumbled ten yards from their campfire. "*Mon frère*!" he cried, glancing over his shoulder in the direction from which the shot had come.

He slid out a blade hanging at his side, lifted it, and plunged it into his gut, ending his own life in the despair that showed in his tragic eyes. Dark fluid spilled onto his jacket as he hit the ground with a thud.

Duncan covered Clarissa's mouth to prevent a scream.

"I apologize." He put his cheek against hers, and her tears wet his face.

They waited for long moments. No one else approached. Duncan helped her up and into the wagon, tucking a blanket around her. She cried quietly in his arms until she fell asleep.

~ * ~

The next day, they washed with wet rags and a piece of soap inside their wagon with the canvas closed around them. They discussed the quiet ride they had taken earlier, farther into Russia. Once done washing, Duncan went into their food and drink supplies.

He passed Clarissa a tin cup of wine and joined her on the seat behind their sturdy horse. "Sweetheart, are you well after what we witnessed yesterday?"

"I'm fine." Pale-faced, she sipped her wine, but she didn't appear recovered from shock of the previously witnessed events.

He wanted to draw her thoughts elsewhere. "Tell me more about your sister-in-law."

"Putting the pieces together with plenty of time to ponder it, and having discussed it with you, I imagine she is Bavarian, though she never told me so—remember her parents insisted she forget her heritage. It was in 1805 when Bavaria entered into an alliance with…" Her tone came out flat.

He reached into a sack in the wagon and withdrew a comb. "Turn around."

She smiled, so he knew he called it right. After removing pins and admiring her tumbling locks, he ran the comb through her hair with long strokes, hoping to soothe her.

She glanced at him over her shoulder. "You don't have to—"

"I want to."

"You favor my hair, Duncan? It's such a mousy brown."

"It's the color of sand, and I like sand."

She chuckled, bringing a smile to his face.

"Napoleon, against Russia and Austria. He rewarded Bavaria by making it a kingdom," he continued offhandedly with the previous subject.

"I wonder if this is important."

He stroked a stray curl. "I'm sure it is an important piece of the puzzle. At this point, though, Clarissa, the pieces we have are too far apart to make a sensible picture."

"Whatever we discover regarding Harriet, I love you."

"I love you too."

~ * ~

With nearby firelight flickering under the lengthening shadows of dusk, Clarissa and Duncan stretched out, side by side.

"It's the twentieth day." She shifted.

"Napoleon thought the war would be concluded by now. He hoped to force the Russians into a major battle. Instead, the Russian army continues to retreat." He traced her frowning lips with his thumb. "What troubles you tonight?"

She rolled over and looked at the sky. "The emperor leading the Grand Armeé into a great unknown, into hell perhaps." She splayed her fingers then rested them on her belly. "What happens when they can't retreat anymore? Is there a trap?"

He faced her. "It's also July fourteenth, the anniversary of the liberation of the Bastille prison."

"The world around us suffocates me."

He thought of the half a million men resting ahead of them. The air hung heavy, as if the world were approaching its end. Thousands of Napoleon's troops had already disappeared, due to fatigue, desertion, hunger, disease, or raids by Russians—soldiers picked off, one by one.

"Napoleon discovered this poor road network." He glanced at the wagon wheel he had to repair. "His advance has to be on a narrow plane, the men advancing without room to spread out, and too many soldiers to supplement supplies by living off the land. The Russians burning the land makes matters worse. We're lucky to find ample food for our horse."

"Duncan, the further we forge ahead inland into this country, the darker the sky seems at night."

He wove his fingers between hers. "I agree."

Scuffling sounds drew his attention. He sat up. Two soldiers straggled nearby. Their uniforms hung on them, and their hollow cheeks made him wince. They disappeared from view behind a stand of trees.

"They are hungry," Clarissa uttered.

"They're the enemy, but oddly, for the first time in my life, I see such men as human beings, like myself. I see their loose uniforms, how weak they look from not having enough food. It disturbs me. It gives me the stark impression that—"

"That what?"

"Soldiers, even enemy soldiers, don't deserve to die this way. I could—"

The explosion of two gunshots interrupted him. Clarissa screamed and jumped into his arms.

"—offer them…food," he uttered tragically, knowing it was too late.

"Oh, Duncan."

He had to change the subject, fast. "That book you've been reading—"

She sniffled and sat up, swiping away her tears. "Is the world ending?" She quivered.

He knew by the innocence in her regard she would believe anything he told her. Warmth seeped into his bones. *So different than the day in your shop when you believed your sister-in-law's word over my judgment.*

"No, Clarissa, of course not." He embraced her. "Do not worry."

She rested against his chest, relieved, it seemed. Peace descended upon his soul as she huddled in the protection of his arms…he, her only source of comfort and sole refuge. A shiver coursed through her. He kissed her, embracing her tighter, willing to do anything to protect her—and grateful, so grateful she had faith in him.

~ * ~

The next night Duncan tried to give Clarissa stew in a tin cup. She pushed it away.

"Clarissa?"

"I can't. I saw a thousand dead horses today."

Images of his thoroughbreds had him glancing down. "I wonder how mine are faring."

"You esteem your horses so much."

"Yes. They're beautiful, powerful creatures. I can't eat supper now." He put down his tin cup.

Clarissa went to him. He tried to calm her trembling limbs, rubbing her arms. The camp kettle of tea came to a boil.

He kissed her and then took the kettle off the fire. "People have tried to kill Napoleon."

"It...seems inevitable."

"Some workmen once tried to replace his snuff box, laced it with poison. Another time, a bomb by his carriage almost took him as he was on his way to the opera."

"I'm grateful you're not an emperor."

~ * ~

Days later, on July 21st, Duncan offered Clarissa his canteen, and she sipped a mouthful of stale water. "Do we have no fresh water?"

"There was so much sickness amongst the troops who camped here, I believe the local water is tainted—that's why we're still using what we took from the lake three days ago."

"I thought those two men stumbling along the track were suffering from ague. The deeper into Russia we go, the more units weaken, and the further the soldiers go in search of food. Their officers are losing control." She gripped her skirt, turning her knuckles white.

"Sweetheart? These roads are so sandy or marshy. This can't end well."

"No, it can't."

"We certainly can't stay to find out what happens."

"Our end of this mass of humanity is getting increasingly disorganized. They don't like the heat."

"I don't either, but it's going to get cold then frigid."

"Have you spoken to your contact?" she asked.

"No, but I intend to soon. We must move further up the line of men and draw closer to the army."

She straightened her spine. "That would be dangerous. The Russians could decide to engage them in battle at any time."

"We'll stay outside of the mass of soldiers and move up along the flank."

"Duncan—"

"Sweetheart, what is it?"

"I no longer care if Harriet was a spy. I did once...the thought distressed me, but now—"

How could he respond? Disappointment, frustration, yet sympathy assailed him.

"I want to go home. Daily, I pine for the green fields around London, and the church bells ringing on a Sunday morning."

He stood. "I'm going to mention your sister-in-law's name casually and see what I can find out. Keep the pistol in clear view."

"I will."

Twenty

The evening of July 25th arrived. Clarissa watched Duncan across the flickering flames of their campfire.

"During my foraging, news came to my attention."

"What?" She sipped water from her canteen.

"It concerns Commander Davout. He and his men were in the south. They surrounded the Russian troops there under Bagration and those intending to join the larger Russian force. Davout cut them off, thank goodness. When he journeyed north, though, Bagration's second army attacked. It's said that Davout's army holds a strong position."

"What were the casualties?"

"Four to one in favor of the French, can you credit it?" he said. "More men lost. Napoleon sent a corps toward St. Petersburg to circle around."

Clarissa took his hand as she did often.

~ * ~

The next day, the smaller group of Napoleon's men took Polotsk. Clarissa and Duncan remained behind the big army. News came to them of the resistance the French contended with when they hit Kliatstitsy. Duncan discussed it with his wife.

Late in the day, he helped her disembark from the wagon, offering her a drink of water. She trembled.

"What is it?"

"I can't forget the screams of dying men, Duncan. They disturbed me."

"Me as well. The surviving men who suffered defeat retreated to Polotsk. Well, once there, they were reinforced, but it wasn't enough to allow them to advance. They were stuck."

After she stretched she climbed back into the wagon. He joined her, and she huddled against him under the canvas flap. He tied it shut.

"Will this army ever make it to Moscow? Soldiers die daily."

"They may, but we won't. I spoke to my contact."

"And?"

"He's heard of her."

She inhaled sharply. "It must be a mistake."

"No. I said 'Harriet,' and he replied with 'Hale.'"

"I don't understand why she'd use her real name."

He shrugged. "I imagine terror addled her senses initially, or she gave it under intense interrogation or..." He didn't want to say that they did worse. "She was only with them for a month."

"Why?"

"Sweetheart?"

She lifted tear-filled eyes to his.

He scrubbed his face. "She came to England in 1799, the year Maximillian ascended the throne of Bavaria—and we have strong reasons to believe she's Bavarian. Napoleon helped Bavaria against the Austrians."

"Yes. But that was years after she became English."

"But it's possible her loyalties remained with her native country, despite the effort of her parents to erase her heritage."

"Conceivably, Duncan. 1809. Bavaria rallied with Napoleon because he had helped them earlier against the Austrians who had attacked them. They were French-controlled. Austria and Russia were allies. And during Harriet's absence last year, tension escalated between France and Russia."

"There's more to this, Clarissa. You're going to have to go home and get the rest from your sister-in-law yourself."

"Why would she tell me?"

"Because I'm not going to denounce her."

"She was never in that hospital. You didn't see my other notes. I have written testimony from Dr. Dearborn. I threatened to go public and scandalize him when I discovered he was Ewan's friend and had fabricated such a lie. He didn't want his career ruined and admitted that he lied to help out an old friend."

"How have you discovered the friendship?"

"I suspected it and told him I located an old letter around the house, signed by him and addressed to Ewan. I told him my lawyer was in possession of it. He broke down and told me everything. To test him, I asked him to tell me something only he and your family would know."

"And did he?"

She regarded him. "Is it true that your father's real name was Darius?"

"Yes, but no one outside of our family knew. His father referred to him as Robert, and so did everyone else."

"Well, Ewan obviously told his friend Dr. Dearborn. What was your father like?"

He scratched his chin. "He—"

"What is it? Was he more like you or Ewan, your other siblings?"

"Me, I suppose. He was a soldier and an entrepreneur. As a young man, he went to Scotland on a business deal for the army. That was where my parents became acquainted. A Highland beauty, as he used to tell it, inspected him with an admiring eye. Her brother was playing the haunting melody 'Lady Anne Bothwell's Lament' on the bagpipes. My mother said she asked him to stop. 'But Evina, it is your favorite song!' Her brother noticed an English soldier watching them. He could hardly believe it. My mother advised him that she thought she was in love. My father approached them and bowed, staring at her."

"How delightful."

Duncan smiled. "For months my father transacted only with the Scottish. He lost money on certain deals, but he didn't care. Courting my mother constituted his most important venture, and he had the influence to do that. When it proved difficult to get her father to agree to the marriage, Father promised to name a child after him. Grudgingly, my grandfather permitted the wedding."

"I'm glad of that." She snuggled against him.

"As am I. So where was Mrs. Hale during the rest of her missing time?"

Clarissa leaned back. "Where do you think she was, bacon brain?"

Frustrated, he prepared a rebuttal, but she tilted her head in question. His heart did a flip, and he kissed her, not expecting such a sudden and deep need to consume him. Floodgates burst open from the continuous gentle pressure of her innocently given love.

They kissed deeply for long moments and removed each other's clothes with loving caresses. His mouth descended upon her soft neck. He gave her a series of tender kisses, touching her, as his spirit dissolved into her loving caresses. Pleasure radiated outward from his center. Gently, he eased her onto their thick blanket, barely able to see her face in the dimness of the canvas surrounding them.

He searched for areas on her skin that would arouse pleasure. She rubbed her legs against him. The heat from her body and her soft mewling sounds sent passion coursing through his veins.

"Duncan, Duncan."

He seared a path down her abdomen and onto her thigh. "Clarissa." He explored the soft surface of her waist and hips. She squirmed beneath him. He kissed and tasted her as he moved over her silken flesh, stroking with the tip of his tongue. She curled into the curve of his body. He trembled, cupping her face, enjoying drafts of air filled with the warm scent of her. She nuzzled her cheek against his hair.

He nudged her knees apart with his. "I love you."

"I love you, too."

He entered her with a thrust, inhaling her sweet essence, moving his hips. The pleasure rose, gaining urgency until it detonated. He gripped her shoulders as he found his release gazing upon her, barely making out the tears that made clear paths down her dirt-smudged cheeks. She traced his jaw.

"Sweetheart?" He wiped away her tears.

"I've waited so long."

"I've missed you so much. You are mine, Clarissa Amberley." He kissed her. Curling the blanket around them, he held her.

~ * ~

The next day, eating their hard breakfast biscuits and sipping coffee, Clarissa considered Duncan. "It's the end of July. Napoleon suffers harassment on his army's flanks?"

"Yes. Then there are the logistics problems. Things are not going as planned. Failed discipline, looting and those things."

"Duncan, he's halted his advance. Everyone rests here. Why don't we return home?"

"Yes, and face what we must."

~ * ~

The long trip back across Russia's burnt terrain in the rickety wagon exhausted them body and soul. August proved to be dusty and dry. For long stretches of time, Duncan and Clarissa trekked through a scene of nightmarish bloodshed. The groans of the dying disturbed their steps. Rural communities lay in ruins.

Duncan knew that Clarissa, like himself, could not leave the scene behind fast enough. Injured, sick, and stragglers flocked to the army's sides and in its rear, many pillaged. Duncan kept a loaded musket within clear view, and his wife clasped her pistol on her lap.

He drew the horse to a stop near a small lake and let his horse drink. Using a bucket dipped into its water, they caught a couple of fish, and boiled them in saltwater, then enjoyed them for dinner. Not wanting to linger, he and Clarissa climbed into their wagon and were off.

They lumbered along in their vehicle, sitting side by side. She glanced over and saw him pondering things while he guided the reins.

"What are you considering so heavily?"

He glanced up at the gray sky and shivered. "How vulnerable I feel."

She grabbed his hand.

"On a ship, in the midst of battle, cannonballs flying, I knew I could die, but this is different."

"How?"

"I was with my men. If we went down, we'd go down believing truth and justice would prevail. Here, it's you and me. Your life is in my hands. And because of my love for you, my life means far more to me now. Anything could happen as we cross this vast terrain of waste. We could be shot from a distance, we could..." He paused again. "If we're approached, and you cannot discern nationality from outerwear, let them speak first. If they're Russian, speak English. Be British."

"I thought as much."

~ * ~

The next few weeks of travel proved difficult. As arduous as this journey had been, at least she spent her days and nights with him. Her throat constricted imagining speaking with Harriet. Near the end of August, her clothes stained and torn in various places, she turned to Duncan.

His face was shadowed with fatigue, and he curled his fingers around hers. "I'm glad we were together for this. We have grown closer through this experience."

"As am I. Harriet was only with Napoleon a short while and with Ewan the rest of the time."

He inhaled deeply. She prepared for a reprimand that did not come.

"Ewan has said and done things that have alarmed me. It's dreadful to think he would do those things your sister-in-law insisted he did."

"I couldn't believe Harriet would be a spy."

"To the devil with them both."

~ * ~

Duncan and Clarissa traveled the gloomy land, scattered with remains and debris, while staying as far from the battlefield as possible. Their dismal expressions and overly sized clothes made them appear half-starved. But in truth, both had lost a few pounds. Soldiers roamed the plane of war, in the midst of masses of corpses. They scavenged their dead colleagues' packs in search of food.

Early September dawned chilly and foggy as Duncan and Clarissa came close to the Russian border, riding along in their wagon. She draped her shoulders with a blanket.

He noted her downturned lips. "Think of home and not the burnt and devastated landscape of this faraway world."

"Yes, enchanting home."

"You're an amazing woman."

Her expression melted into one of tenderness. "Duncan?"

"You were put in a terrifying situation, and you did not break. You kept your cover and your wits about you the entire time. I'm proud of you, Clarissa." He regarded her warmly.

"I'm glad. I would not want to shame my husband."

"You don't."

"I was terrified, but when fear threatened to overcome me, I turned and looked at you. If I am to be worthy of a man like you, then I could not feed a proclivity to weakness. I could not allow myself to crumble. I discovered strength I didn't know I had. And it's because of you."

He kissed her fingers. "In my den, working, I will think of holding you under a massive black sky with countess stars twinkling above us. I will remember looking into your beautiful dirt-smudged, courageous face, as I made love to you. I will remember walking by your side, aware of inner strength emanating from you thinking, 'You truly are my soul mate.'"

She kissed him. Rain spattered onto his face. A glance up at the gray sky told him to expect more than a drizzle. He helped her under the canvas covering.

~ * ~

At the end of September, they finally stepped off the stagecoach in Charing Cross, London. Duncan hired a cab for the short journey to the Hale Emporium. He deposited an exhausted Clarissa there, so she could get cleaned up and gather her bags. A 'closed' sign hung on the shop door.

"I'm truly and deeply regretful we discovered what we did. You'll never comprehend how much so," Duncan said.

Tears rolled down her cheeks. He searched his pockets for his handkerchief and retrieved the tattered cloth before stopping short of wiping her cheeks. "Sorry dear. It's ruined."

She grabbed it, using it to wipe her face. "After what we've been through, it's rather nice!"

He looked at her tenderly but with serious intent. "Talk to her. Find out why. Then tell me, please."

"Yes."

He tipped her chin up and kissed her. "At supper tonight. We will enjoy a decent meal."

"Goodbye, husband. I'll see you soon." She grabbed his hand before unlocking the door.

"Tonight, Clarissa. Come home."

Her hand slid from his as he hesitantly let go. Her fingers tingled where his had been. She stepped inside and watched from the window as his hired carriage disappeared down the road. She went upstairs, expecting her mother, Marian, to have returned from her holiday. Marian opened the door to her rooms, and they embraced. They chatted for a while. Marian had a gentle voice, and Clarissa lowered the volume of her own nearly to a whisper conversing with her mother.

Later, Clarissa threw off her grubby traveling gown and kicked it aside. She stepped into a bath of hot water with an "Ahhh" as steam rose around her. She picked up a piece of lye soap, looking at it. *In Duncan's home, the soap is finer and smells of lavender.* She shrugged. *It does not signify. It's soap.*

She sat soaking, washing her hair and scrubbing her skin. Marian helped empty the tub then aided her in arranging her hair. She sent her daughter across to the rooms above the shop, to the right, where Harriet conversed with Gilbert in their own rooms.

After she embraced Gilbert and Harriet, they sat. Clarissa inhaled slowly, reluctant to launch into her story. In a hand cold with anxiety, she grabbed Gilbert's and in the other, Harriet's. "Brother, sister, I have much on my mind."

She told her tale of her and Duncan's travels behind Napoleon's army. Harriet shifted in her stuffed chair. Gilbert's features revealed his puzzlement.

His brows drawn in question, he asked, "Why were you and Duncan spies? Did our Prince Regent call him to duty?"

"No."

"Then why?"

"Duncan had to find out for himself. Not that he's going to do anything with the information. He's prepared to live with it."

"What information?" Gilbert stared. Bafflement covered his apprehensive face.

She began thickly, "Harriet, Duncan and I encountered your name there."

Harriet bounded to her feet. She slumped her shoulders over the table behind her as if the world rested upon them.

Gilbert stood, touching her back. "Harriet, sweetheart, what is it?"

She turned around. "After Mr. Amberley abducted me—well, I never thought you would find out. I did not want you ever to find out." Her voice was emotionless, monotonous, and it chilled Clarissa.

Harriet's gaze rose to meet theirs. "I escaped finally and ran for the docks. A ship prepared to leave. Mr. Amberley was close behind me."

Gilbert listened wide-eyed, hearing these details for the first time.

"I had no choice. He was close. Would have caught me."

Clarissa was hearing the undeniable and dreadful facts. Questions hammered her. She remained silent, listening, and waited to hear her explanation for treason.

As Harriet continued, Clarissa's throat constricted with sadness.

"I hid on the ship and wasn't exposed until it was too late for them to put me off. I sailed with them to Spain, and they fed me sufficiently."

Clarissa interrupted. "The British helped the Spanish against Napoleon—the Peninsular War."

"Only hours after I stepped off the ship, wandering around in search of more food, a couple of Napoleon's men grabbed me. Clarissa, I remembered a little of the French you taught me. I knew enough to communicate to them that I'd cooperate. They informed me they could find a use for me and brought me to Napoleon. He questioned me on my origins.

"I spoke in French, terrified. The word 'English' would not find itself past my lips. I uttered that I was 'Bavarian.' His mouth curved up in approval. 'So your countrymen are grateful to me?'" She twisted her hands. "Oh, he was perfectly polite, but underlying threat spilled from his silky voice."

"Frightening," Clarissa uttered.

"Indeed," Harriet said. "I told him, yes, we were grateful, that we profited when he defeated Austria. He gave me a slow nod, seemingly staring into my soul." She shivered. "Napoleon said, 'Bavaria rallied with me once again two years ago.' 'Yes,' I squeaked out. 'I believe in and support our alliance.' He continued in that falsely gentle tone. 'But you were with the British?' 'I...allowed myself to be captured. My father has rank in the Bavarian army,' I lied. 'It was my intention to make the British believe I had turned, so I could plant misinformation.' 'You're a spy?' 'Yes,' I answered him." She hiccupped, her pink cheeks displaying her agitation.

Twisting a yellow ribbon from her gown and looking down, she continued. "I could feel him glowering at me. He asked my name, and I had no power over my own tongue to give him anything but the truth."

"But you lied about other things," Clarissa said.

"You weren't there," Harriet said. "I wasn't in my right mind. Fear brings things out. Anyway, he waved dismissively. He told me he could find a use for me and my French was passable, not perfect, but my fluent English would be useful. He would spare me. I thanked him. I never did anything that caused the death of another person."

Clarissa reeled backwards in shock. "You really had no choice."

"No."

"Duncan will keep his silence. Do not fear," Gilbert said.

She bowed her head over slumped shoulders.

"Do you hate me, Gilbert, Clarissa?"

"No," Gilbert stated.

"No," Clarissa uttered with regret. She'd grown up with Harriet and knew what she spoke was true.

"How did you get away from him?"

Gilbert's quiet voice contained an undertone of anxiety.

"In the chaos of war, it didn't prove too difficult. As cannon balls flew and firearms shot off, as screams tore through the air and smoke and blood spurted everywhere, I zigzagged behind horses, trees, boulders, and whatever I could find.

"I made my way running to the docks and got on another ship. I hid, covered in blankets, shivering inside the tightest little space I could find. I ended up in England, confused."

"And wandering around Union Street," Clarissa added.

"Yes." Harriet regarded her endearingly.

"I understand. Thank you," Clarissa said.

Harriet nodded. "Since that day I ran from Mr. Amberley, I've been going back and forth between fear and sadness and anger. Sometimes I still feel like a victim, but often I suffer anger, and I'm able to do something about it due to my extraordinary experiences working under Napoleon. Go and tell Duncan. Maybe he will understand."

Clarissa looked skyward. "One can only hope and pray. It would give him much comfort."

"Good luck, sister." Gilbert patted her shoulder.

She stood with determination.

~ * ~

Clarissa trembled in anticipation during the ride to Duncan's home. She stepped from the carriage and glimpsed from side to side to assure herself Duncan's brother was not in attendance. She walked up the wide, welcoming staircase with flutters in her belly. When the butler went to retrieve Duncan, she stopped him.

"The younger Mr. Amberley is not here?"

"No. He has left the premises on the captain's orders."

"Thank you," she said, relieved, but worried. Would Mr. Amberley try to hurt them?

She coiled a lace cloth with her gloved hands while awaiting her husband and glanced into a large gilded mirror, hoping her appearance would be pleasing to him.

A matching long autumn pelisse of a chestnut brown and a shimmering silk dress adorned her and caught the light as she moved. Her hair hung in long ringlets in the style of the ancient Greeks. She permitted herself a smile of self-approval. The sound of footsteps clicking on polished wood interrupted her reverie. She looked up and inhaled sharply. He had dressed up, too.

Her darling husband wore a fine white linen shirt and cravat, light-colored pantaloons, and shiny Hessians. His coat was cut to fit him perfectly. Beneath it was a waistcoat of embroidered yellow silk. A black ribbon held his dark, normally unruly hair tied back neatly. His well-groomed appearance seemed inconsistent with his suntanned skin.

He drank her in. "You are entrancing, Clarissa."

She took a step toward him, anxiously, but then stopped, checking her enthusiasm.

His lips curved into a smile. He stepped to her. "Do not be hesitant with me, wife." He tipped her chin up with his finger.

"Hello," she said.

He led her to the dining room, alight with a few candles. The silverware caught gleams from the wavering flames. She noted the fine linen.

"I dismissed the servants. We're alone and can talk openly." He watched her with love, drawing a shiver of excitement from her.

"After months of army rations on a burnt frontier under the night sky, I thought you would appreciate a feast: oyster sauce, fish, soup, vegetables, boiled beef, and that is merely the first course. We shall have creams and pastry, game, and so much more," he said with cheer. "Champagne, my lady?"

"Duncan—"

He feathered his fingers against her temples. "Hmm. No dirt smudges to wipe off. You were so adorable with a splotch of mud here," he touched her nose, "or a splotch there." He moved a strand of hair off her face.

She kissed him with tenderness.

"Are you hungry?"

"Could we talk first?"

"Yes." He took her by the elbow, guiding her to the table.

She thanked him when he slid the chair out for her, and then sat himself, drawing his seat close. "You spoke to your sister-in-law?"

She fiddled with a spoon, moving it to the right. "Yes."

"She told you why?"

"Yes."

He sighed. "Why?"

"Oh, Duncan." She enlightened him.

At one point, he held his chin. Later he leaned forward, in avid interest. He kept silent the entire time.

"And as you can see, she had no choice."

His brows were in a straight line.

"Say something."

He grasped the armrests of his chair and rose to his feet. She did as well.

"Whether or not she felt she had no choice, she still committed treason."

"Tell me, do you want Harriet to be punished harshly?"

"No, I do not. I merely do not wish to be untrue to all I hold dear."

"Which is worse, treason or abduction and murder? At least her treason was forced!" She twirled away from him.

He grabbed her wrist and spun her round to face him. "On a ship—it was my first battle as a captain—I fought so hard I did not even stop to think. I had to win. Losing would have meant death for my crew and shame for England."

"Why do you bring this up now?"

"Can you imagine how much I wanted to win that battle?"

"Yes," she uttered.

"I want you more than anything I have ever wanted in my life. I implore you, don't go."

Overcome, she remained silent. Tears threatened to fall. She stepped close to him.

"Sup with me, my love," he asked.

"Yes. And we shall not bring up the subject of relatives."

~ * ~

The next morning, she rolled over in his luxurious bed, so happy to be home with him where she belonged. He draped his arm over her.

She gave him a quick kiss. "I love you. I always will."

He held her close, and she curled against him. They slept for another hour before dressing and going down to breakfast, sharing laughter during their meal.

"You're delightful, Clarissa."

She sipped her rich coffee, shivering with how delicious it was, and winked at him.

He scoffed playfully. "At least you're aware of your attributes."

She gave him a bright smile. "Yes, I have fine taste in gentlemen!"

~ * ~

On the first of October, Duncan arrived at Clarissa's shop on busy Oxford Street and stood in front of its bay window. Wrapping his coat tighter around him, he shivered and inhaled the chilly, damp evening air then glanced about the way. Coal smoke scented the air, and the clippity-clop of horses' hooves sounded around him. He prepared to take his beloved wife home, thinking of her and longing for her as she attended business with her brother. Seeing her keep shop was not something he relished, but he'd die before he complained, perceiving the light it brought to her. He could have sent a carriage for her but chose not to. He'd see her sooner this way.

Duncan peered into the window. Gilbert rested his elbows on the main counter, his cheek in his hand, listening to his sister's words avidly. Clarissa gestured to emphasize the importance of what she read.

Duncan entered her enchanting little business, and the siblings smiled. "Hello," he said to both.

They greeted him.

He tossed a glance at the books and other items resting on the oak shelves, then at the newspaper in his wife's grasp. "What is the story of interest today? Let me guess. The bulk of the British Navy is fighting

Napoleon's men. We only have eleven ships on the line, thirty-four frigates, and about the same number of smaller vessels in the western Atlantic. No more could be spared for the American war."

"It doesn't say that," Gilbert said. "You're retired. How are you cognizant of so much?"

"Regular meetings with officials as a consultant, and I help the regent at times on a personal level. He keeps me informed about what my countrymen are doing out there on the battlefront."

"Interesting," Gilbert said.

Duncan looked at them smiling. "The following information is highly classified, but I trust you both."

Slightly awed, they tipped forward in anticipation.

"Our navy is escorting British merchant shipping, blockading American ports, let's see, protecting the St. Lawrence River, and also, to my dismay, hunting down American frigates."

Clarissa grinned smartly. "I doubt that information is highly classified, husband."

He winked.

"I only wish it were happy news we are currently reading," Gilbert said. "She was so anxious she wouldn't even let me have a peek. She reads to me of the war with America."

"I am greatly disturbed by this war," Duncan said.

The siblings nodded.

"So, how is business?" They could discuss war later.

"Good, thank you," Gilbert said. "But a bit of a slow day today. They'll be in tomorrow. We usually get rushes, then nothing for a couple of hours. A straggler or two later."

Duncan scanned the quiet room before turning to his wife and her sibling. "Since Clarissa and I have reconciled our differences, I'd like to tell you two something of my past, something that has kept me up nights."

Clarissa put the newspaper down on the counter. "About the Navy?"

"No. My family."

Twenty-one

Clarissa and Gilbert gave Duncan their full attention, leaning onto the counter.

"I'd like to discuss the family I lost."

Clarissa reached out and caressed his fingers. Love curled through him.

"James, the second-born, served in the army. He died in battle whilst I was away in service."

She slipped her fingers around his in a reassuring squeeze, then let go.

He responded with a fleeting thanks. "One day, approximately a year later, a new recruit joined my crew on the ship. I recognized him as the brother of a woman my eldest brother Ned had loved. The man told me his sister regretted leaving Ned and wished to accept his marriage proposal after serious thought, but sadly, in the process of returning to him, she perished in an accident."

"Duncan, that is distressing."

Gilbert shook his head. "What happened?"

"I wrote to Ned and told him. He was sickly as a child and into adulthood...his heart, you see. It seems he had had a trying week and lay bedridden at the time he received my letter. Ewan gave it to him, hoping it might cheer him. Ned read the letter with Ewan still in the room. Ned suffered a seizure of the heart and died. Ewan scanned the letter and blamed me for killing our weakened brother."

"No," Clarissa muttered.

"Tell him." Gilbert nudged her.

"Tell me what?"

"You could use a bit of cheer after that story." He looked at his sister. "Earlier, she felt not quite well, so I took her to see the doctor. We only returned moments before you arrived."

He frowned, confused. "What? Clarissa, why didn't you send a note?"

"You told me you expected to travel today to discuss business with a colleague."

"Someone would have located me. I leave my intended whereabouts with a servant in case such a need arises, especially now that I'm married. What happened at the doctor's office?"

Gilbert shrugged. "I do apologize. You should have heard this first, but I refused to leave the room when the doctor said he had a diagnosis. Forgive me for hearing this before you."

"Never mind." He turned to Clarissa. "Darling, tell me."

A glow came to her face. She walked around the counter, faced him directly, and gestured. "Let's discuss this over there."

He guided her to a private corner by a bookshelf. She whispered into his ear.

He glanced at her belly. "Oh, darling, that's delightful!"

"There's something regarding my family I never told you."

"Something happy, I presume."

"Something interesting. Both of our parents are twins."

"What?" He darted a look across at Gilbert.

Gilbert busied himself with moving inventory from a box to a shelf, paying them no attention.

"Yes," she began. "Our father lost his twin brother as a boy, and our mother's twin sister lives in Ireland with her husband. Chances are high, Duncan, that I'll give you two children at a time. We might have many children but with only half the breeding time."

He embraced her. The bell at the door tinkled, and he drew away, smiling hugely. A young couple strolled in, and Gilbert greeted them.

Duncan turned to Clarissa. "I think I shall look through your fine selection of books and supplies. I'd like to make a large purchase in celebration of the best news I have ever received."

"Well, good, sir," she teased, "explore at your leisure." She resumed her position behind the counter.

He went to the opposite end of the room, elated with the prospect of becoming a father. His attention landed on a stack of books from the previous century.

The door tore open and with it, a burst of frigid air. A masked man strode in. He reached under his coat and exposed a crimson waistcoat. Out came a pistol. The female patron gasped, and the man with her dragged her to the floor and covered her with his body.

The masked man lifted his arm and pointed his weapon directly at Clarissa's chest. Duncan leapt, aiming for the path of the gun. Too far away to tackle the gunman, he didn't make it as the shot exploded. He twisted as the gun went off and looked at Clarissa. She fell into Gilbert's arms. He lowered her to the floor.

Duncan ran to her side and crouched, shaking. "Clarissa!" But a quick scan of her chest revealed no blood.

She blinked. "Help me."

Gilbert looked at her back. "There is no wound here."

Duncan studied her. "Darling?"

"I fainted."

He chuckled in joy but stopped short and turned a sharp eye to see the shooter, but from his crouched position behind the counter, he could not see him.

Gilbert distracted Duncan by gripping his arm briefly. "Thank God. Had it been...I was only close enough to catch her as she fell," Gilbert said.

"Gilbert attempted to jump in front of me." Clarissa's voice shook. "What happened? Where is the shooter? Did he run away?"

The rustle of the curtain drew their attention. The three of them turned.

Harriet stood there with a wicked gleam in her eyes, holding Gilbert's pistol. "I'm finally free," she cried.

Duncan helped Clarissa into a sitting position then went around the counter. The masked man lay on the ground, unmoving, blood oozing from the center of his chest. Duncan stopped suddenly then approached with caution, but he sensed the man was dead. He prodded the villain's side with his foot. Still he didn't move, so Duncan bent and removed the mask. Ewan lay there, unmoving. Duncan gasped, inched himself up, and regarded Mrs. Hale.

"I saw his carriage as I glanced out the window, which I do often," she said, "and came downstairs to warn you and Clarissa, worrying he'd hurt you. Taking up Gilbert's pistol that a military friend gifted him, I intended on scaring that criminal away. I opened the curtain as he prepared to kill Clarissa. Hmm. When the man took me, he wore a crimson waistcoat like that which Mr. Amberley wears now. It's distinct with the gold trimming on one side and silver on the other, and I'll wager if you check, the one on him has the same markings."

"Yes," Duncan said. He had seen it, and it did.

Mrs. Hale smiled at Clarissa. "Now you understand why I do not paint with red."

A male patron spoke up. "My wife and I witnessed everything." He brought his attention to Mrs. Hale. "You saved the shopkeeper's life."

Duncan immediately forgave Mrs. Hale her transgressions, as the weight of bearing her secret of treason lifted from his soul.

~ * ~

A week later, sitting in front of the hearth in Duncan's room, Clarissa took Duncan's hand.

"I must ask. What about your brother? What are you feeling?"

Duncan brushed a strand of hair from her forehead. His brow narrowed in a fleeting show of anger. "He tried to kill you."

"But—"

"I'll rein in my anger, and say, 'May he rest in peace.' He never had it here. My mother took his passing poorly, but now her life will be without worry."

"You're quite well?"

"Yes. I respect and am fond of Gilbert as my own blood brother. I like him more than I ever liked Ewan, I'm ashamed to say. Ewan troubled me deeply. I was not a free man but trapped by a responsibility for a person without a conscience. However, I regret not being able to help him."

"Don't be ashamed. He was not a good man."

Duncan sighed. "I've grown because of my feelings for you."

"How is that possible?"

"My habit of denial is over. I was afraid to face the truth about Ewan."

"Battle didn't frighten you."

"No. There were several people at once to go up against. I did not have to face their personal truths."

~ * ~

Months later, Duncan cradled a precious baby in each arm, close to his sides. He kissed their foreheads. "My babies, my darling babies. I love you so much, Harriet and Jillian."

He gently placed the babies into their cribs in the nursery and covered them with fluffy blankets. His arm came around his wife's side, pulling her against him.

"They love you, Duncan. Their little cries stopped while you cradled them against your chest, safe in your arms. They fell so peacefully asleep in their father's loving arms."

"They have eyes the color of a turquoise stone."

"And dark hair like their father, as in my vision. Come my love, our waiting period is complete."

He led her to his bedroom and kissed her madly. "You've made such a difference in my life."

"You have changed my life too."

"It was my pleasure. I will love you deeply, energetically, and forever, Clarissa," and he affirmed his promise with a kiss.

Meet Lara MacGregor

Lara MacGregor lives in Colorado and enjoys the great beauty the state has to offer. She has written flash fiction to full-length novels. Her work is mostly historical but includes other genres as well, such as paranormal and especially time travel stories. She has a B.A. in Modern Languages (French emphasis) with a minor in music and an M.A. in history. Lara's Master's thesis was on the War of 1812. She plays guitar and piano and loves reading as many books as time will allow.

Other Works From The Pen Of
Lara MacGregor

The 12th Kiss- In 19th century London, she can fight and becomes a hero. He falls in love with her. His biggest mistake is to demand she stop her activities.

The Mask of Truth, book One - A prince accused of murder must prove his innocence, save his country from a tyrant, and win over his true love's heart or lose all.

War Between Brother Kings - The Mask of Truth, Book Two - A prince must face off with his dangerous brother, a king, to save millions and even his own family. The king gets creative.

Letter to Our Readers

Enjoy this book?

You can make a difference

As an independent publisher, Wings ePress, Inc. does not have the financial clout of the large New York Publishers. We can't afford large magazine spreads or subway posters to tell people about our quality books.

But, we do have something much more effective and powerful than ads. We have a large base of loyal readers.

Honest Reviews help bring the attention of new readers to our books.

If you enjoyed this book, we would appreciate it if you would spend a few minutes posting a review on the site where you purchased this book or on the Wings ePress, Inc. webpages at: https://wingsepress. com/

Visit Our Website

For The Full Inventory
Of Quality Books:

Wings ePress.Inc
https://wingsepress.com/

Quality trade paperbacks and downloads
in multiple formats,
in genres ranging from light romantic comedy
to general fiction and horror.
Wings has something for every reader's taste.
Visit the website, then bookmark it.
We add new titles each month!

Wings ePress Inc.
3000 N. Rock Road
Newton, KS 67114